Do You Feel Lucky?

Slocum turned to keep the two rustlers on his left at bay, only to find that his Winchester came up empty. Using his Colt Navy, he gained himself a few seconds and hunted for the shining brass cartridges that had fallen on the dry canyon bottom. He rolled behind a boulder and stuffed the four rounds he had retrieved into the Winchester. A quick look around didn't reveal any more rounds of ammo.

"We got 'im, boys. Charge!"

Slocum heard the command from his right side. A quick glance confirmed what this really meant. He whirled left and got off all four shots from the rifle before coming up empty. As the hammer fell on the empty chamber, a wry smile crossed his face. Four shots and he had brought down two of the outlaws.

He turned back to the other direction as those rustlers advanced. And from the corner of his eye he saw three others advancing from the depths of the canyon.

All he had left were a couple rounds in his six-gun. He vowed to make them count.

DON'T MISS THESE
ALL-ACTION WESTERN SERIES
FROM THE BERKLEY PUBLISHING GROUP

THE GUNSMITH by J. R. Roberts
Clint Adams was a legend among lawmen, outlaws, and ladies. They called him . . . the Gunsmith.

LONGARM by Tabor Evans
The popular long-running series about Deputy U.S. Marshal Custis Long—his life, his loves, his fight for justice.

SLOCUM by Jake Logan
Today's longest-running action Western. John Slocum rides a deadly trail of hot blood and cold steel.

BUSHWHACKERS by B. J. Lanagan
An action-packed series by the creators of Longarm! The rousing adventures of the most brutal gang of cutthroats ever assembled—Quantrill's Raiders.

DIAMONDBACK by Guy Brewer
Dex Yancey is Diamondback, a Southern gentleman turned con man when his brother cheats him out of the family fortune. Ladies love him. Gamblers hate him. But nobody pulls one over on Dex . . .

WILDGUN by Jack Hanson
The blazing adventures of mountain man Will Barlow—from the creators of Longarm!

TEXAS TRACKER by Tom Calhoun
J.T. Law: the most relentless—and dangerous—manhunter in all Texas. Where sheriffs and posses fail, he's the best man to bring in the most vicious outlaws—for a price.

JAKE LOGAN

SLOCUM
AND THE
DEVIL'S ROPE

JOVE BOOKS, NEW YORK

THE BERKLEY PUBLISHING GROUP
Published by the Penguin Group
Penguin Group (USA) Inc.
375 Hudson Street, New York, New York 10014, USA
Penguin Group (Canada), 90 Eglinton Avenue East, Suite 700, Toronto, Ontario M4P 2Y3, Canada
(a division of Pearson Penguin Canada Inc.) • Penguin Books Ltd., 80 Strand, London WC2R 0RL,
England • Penguin Group Ireland, 25 St. Stephen's Green, Dublin 2, Ireland (a division of Penguin
Books Ltd.) • Penguin Group (Australia), 250 Camberwell Road, Camberwell, Victoria 3124, Australia
(a division of Pearson Australia Group Pty. Ltd.) • Penguin Books India Pvt. Ltd., 11 Community
Centre, Panchsheel Park, New Delhi—110 017, India • Penguin Group (NZ), 67 Apollo Drive,
Rosedale, Auckland 0632, New Zealand (a division of Pearson New Zealand Ltd.) • Penguin Books
(South Africa) (Pty.) Ltd., 24 Sturdee Avenue, Rosebank, Johannesburg 2196, South Africa

Penguin Books Ltd., Registered Offices: 80 Strand, London WC2R 0RL, England

This is a work of fiction. Names, characters, places, and incidents either are the product of the author's
imagination or are used fictitiously, and any resemblance to actual persons, living or dead, business
establishments, events, or locales is entirely coincidental.

SLOCUM AND THE DEVIL'S ROPE

A Jove Book / published by arrangement with the author

PRINTING HISTORY
Jove edition / July 2012

ISBN: 978-0-515-15100-8

JOVE®
Jove Books are published by The Berkley Publishing Group,
a division of Penguin Group (USA) Inc.,
375 Hudson Street, New York, New York 10014.
JOVE® is a registered trademark of Penguin Group (USA) Inc.
The "J" design is a trademark of Penguin Group (USA) Inc.

PRINTED IN THE UNITED STATES OF AMERICA

10 9 8 7 6 5 4 3 2 1

ALWAYS LEARNING   **PEARSON**

1

The circling buzzards worried Tom Garvin. He rubbed his grimy neck and then took off his bandanna. It was soaked with sweat and did nothing to mop up the rivers flowing from his face. He tied the faded red polka-dot cloth back around his neck and twisted in the saddle to get a better look at the carrion eaters. They wheeled downward, every circuit in the air bringing them closer to the ground.

"Somethin' sure as hell's died," he said to himself. He patted his scrawny horse's neck and got an asthmatic snort in return that told him the buzzards would be coming for them soon enough if they stayed out in the hot sun much longer.

But there wasn't anything else he could do. He had to find the beeves that had wandered off or Mr. Magnuson would be sore. The owner of the Bar M Ranch didn't suffer fools or slackers easily, and Tom Garvin wasn't either. Leastways, he didn't think of himself that way. The only reason he had so much trouble tracking the strays from the herd was inexperience. He was barely eighteen and had never punched cattle before.

Raised on a wheat farm in Kansas, he'd had contact with only one cow before—the old milker his pa had. He wasn't ever allowed to go near the bull kept in its own pen some distance away, so his experience came in getting kicked as he tried to pull some milk out of chary teats. After the cow died and his pa died and the tax collector took the farm, there hadn't been anything left for him but to drift westward.

He was damned glad Mr. Magnuson had taken on a greenhorn like him, and he tried his best to keep up with the other hands. The dour one—John Slocum, by name— tried to help with some suggestions now and again, but understanding what he meant was hard. He had no experience at all riding, much less herding cattle. The swayback nag he rode was part of the ranch remuda. Nobody who needed a horse wanted the bag of bones. It was as much an outcast as he was, and that formed some kinship between him and the horse.

Garvin imagined the horse felt a similar bond, but he'd be lying to himself if he ever thought on it too long. The horse wanted to be fed, wanted to be watered, and didn't care about much else, especially being ridden across the rugged landscape in the foothills burning with midday sun.

The buzzards let out another screech and dipped lower. Garvin reached back and touched the stock of his rifle, the one loaned him by Slocum. He couldn't afford a sidearm, and didn't much mind not having three pounds of iron weighing down his hip. He wouldn't know how to use it anyway. On the farm, he had grown up with a rifle pulled in to his shoulder and taking potshots at rabbits and varmints. In lean times, them prairie dogs hadn't tasted all that bad. A bit like kerosene at times, but better than letting his belly think his throat had been slit.

Slocum had told him to sling the rifle scabbard so the stock poked backward. That kept it from getting tangled in brush. He reached back and slid the rifle out and brought it to his shoulder, sighting along the barrel to take a bead on one of the buzzards. His horse bucked at that instant, causing his finger to slip on the trigger. A round discharged, spooking the horse even more and causing it to bolt.

Garvin flailed about for a moment, settling the rifle and grabbing the reins and doing what he could to control the headlong rush—straight for the spot where the buzzards showed the most interest.

By the time he fought the horse to a stop, he saw the reason for the hungry vultures' interest. An oak tree, flagged by the wind coming over the western foothills, had one sturdy branch. Dangling from it swung a man with his hands fastened behind his back and a noose secured around his neck. Even from fifty yards away, Garvin knew the man was very dead.

"Go on, shoo!" He waved his arm in the air, but the buzzards paid no heed. The boldest of the flock landed on the limb above the hanged man and took a tentative snap at tender, putrefying flesh.

Working to keep his horse steady, Garvin got off another shot. He missed the buzzard by a couple inches, but the passage of hot lead so near its ugly head caused the huge bird to take to wing. It didn't have enough drop to get wind under its wings and ended up hopping along on the ground, flapping its wings and letting Garvin know how ill treated it was having its meal disturbed. A second shot did more than disturb the vulture. It left the feathered carcass flopped out on the ground for others to cannibalize.

He trotted to where the wind swung the dead man around. Garvin held down his gorge. He had seen dead men before. His pa had died from the flu, and it hadn't been pretty. But his tongue hadn't lolled out, black and drawing flies. His eyes hadn't bugged out of their sockets, and his face had never been livid with blood that no longer flowed through veins.

When he got his bile under control, Garvin looked closer. The man had been stripped down to his long johns. Even his clothes had been taken along with his boots. Road agents wouldn't have bothered hanging whoever they robbed. A bullet and that would have done the deed.

"What'd you do to piss off the folks what did this to you?" Garvin wondered aloud. His horse turned its head and glared at him. Then it walked a few steps closer so it would be in the dubious shade afforded by the hanging tree. Garvin didn't fight it over this. Being out of the sun suited him, too. He had been too confounded by the dead man to realize what the horse did immediately.

He dismounted, shoved his rifle back into the saddle sheath, and then tethered the horse to a low branch that was hardly a twig growing from the side of the oak. Horse no longer a worry, he went to the man and looked up. The limb was just barely high enough so the man's feet didn't touch the dirt. In his mind's eye he pictured how the man had been put on horseback, the limb hardly above his head. The fall had been a short one. Garvin didn't bother to see if the man's neck had been broke or if he had swung there long enough to choke to death. Either was a lousy way to die.

"They coulda buried you at least," Garvin said. He stepped back and looked at the rope circling the dead man's neck. "Now ain't that 'bout the most expensive rope you ever did see?"

The rope was made from some material he didn't recognize, maybe just hemp turned black from old age, but it carried silver threads throughout that made it distinctive. Garvin had never seen anything like it before, but then he hadn't seen much of ranch life yet. This might be rope favored by the old-timers. Somebody had favored it enough to use as a noose.

He drew his knife and closed the distance to the corpse, his nose wrinkling from the first onset of decay. The man hadn't been swung here for more than a few hours or the buzzards would have spotted him earlier. Hopping up, he slashed with his knife to cut through the rope. His sharp blade bounced off the rope as if he had tried to sever steel. Grumbling, he tried again. And again his knife refused to bite.

Garvin considered leaving the man where he swung, then knew that wasn't the Christian thing to do. No matter what crime he had committed, the man deserved to be buried where the vultures wouldn't rip at his flesh. He went to the tree trunk and shinnied up, going out on the limb until he was just above the body. The rope had been wrapped repeatedly around the gnarled limb, as if the tree were as much hanged as the man. Pressing his knife edge down hard, he sawed back and forth.

The rope refused to yield.

Garvin worked harder and finally gave up when sweat caused him to lose his grip on the knife, and it went tumbling to the ground. Rocking back, he studied the situation, then decided the only way to get the man down was to unwrap the rope, get the knot untied, and then tend to the sorry business of a burial.

It took him the better part of a half hour to uncurl the stiff rope from around the limb and lower the body. He jumped down, crouched beside the dead man, and worked the silver-chased black rope out of the flesh, where it had cut in deep. Garvin shook the rope free and was puzzled when the gore flew off, as if the rope repelled the blood. Tentatively running his hand over the part of the rope that had been around the man's neck didn't show even dampness from the blood. In fact, there was no trace of skin or blood on the rope at all.

He stood and stepped back, the rope dangling in his grip. A slow smile came to his lips. He had thought the rope was stiff. It moved like a snake in his hands. Garvin wasn't much at twirling, not like the others in the company, but he found it easy enough to spin a decent loop. He turned around, widened the loop, and found himself performing tricks the like of which he had never seen even in the traveling Wild West

Show that had come to Liberal when he and his pa happened to be in town.

Laughing, he stepped through the spinning loop and hopped back, lifted it over his head, and was enjoying himself when he heard a whinny. Garvin let the rope drop to the ground as he stared at a sleek, well-groomed chestnut mare watching from a distance.

"Now who might you be?" He hefted the rope and began walking slowly toward the skittish horse. It wasn't saddled but had been ridden recently from the lather on its flanks. "Might it be you were the one responsible for him taking his last drop?" That the mare belonged to the dead man seemed likely. A mustang would never come by itself so close to any man without putting up more of a fuss.

A twist of his wrist brought a small loop to the end of the black rope. When he began spinning it overhead, the horse stopped and stared, as if mesmerized by the flash of silver threads amid the black. Garvin let fly. The loop closed over the chestnut horse's neck. It reared, and he found himself fighting to keep from being dragged behind it. But he succeeded in tugging enough on the rope, shortening the length, and finally getting the horse to keep all four hooves on the ground.

Garvin patted the horse's neck. Unlike the scrawny reject from a glue factory that he rode, the horse didn't mind. It nuzzled him and playfully bumped at him with her head.

"You're mine, I reckon," Garvin said. The horse didn't argue.

But first he had to finish the chore he had started. The ground was hard and the grave ended up shallower than he would have liked, but Tom Garvin laid the hanged man to rest.

2

Being alone on the trail gave John Slocum time to think. He had found a half-dozen scrawny strays and slowly herded them back toward the Bar M pens, where they would be fattened a mite before returning to the main herd. Pickings were scarce this time of year, and it wasn't long before the trail drive to the railhead began. Slocum had worked for Magnuson most of the year and enjoyed the notion of a steady paycheck and three squares a day. The Bar M might not be the biggest ranch around or the most prosperous, but it provided better employment than Slocum had had in a couple years.

"Get along now," he said, using the tip of his lariat to swat a balky steer on the hindquarter. The bovine's protesting moan had no effect on him. He had heard such sorrow in a cow's lowing too many times to pay it any mind. All he wanted was to get back to the ranch.

He had more than three squares and a paycheck waiting, and that was what set him to thinking on the lonely ride. Christine Magnuson was a mighty fine filly, and she and Slocum had taken to each other like a duck takes to water.

She was spirited and a bit flighty at times, but he found that to his liking. She wasn't what he'd call beautiful, but she was far from ugly. Definitely pretty. Very pretty, even though her nose had been busted when she was growing up a tomboy on the ranch and her pa hadn't set it quite right. But Slocum thought that gave her character. It wasn't as if she were a barroom brawler who'd had his nose broken one time too many or had cauliflower ears from bare-knuckle fights.

In fact, her shell-like ears were downright attractive. As was her midnight dark hair and blazing blue eyes and the tiny smile that curled her bow-shaped lips and the dimples that formed and—

Slocum shook himself out of the reverie because he topped a rise not a quarter mile from the ranch house. Why dream when he could get the real thing in the flesh?

He kept the beeves moving. Whether the promise of fodder or the smell of water moved them faster, he couldn't tell, but he no longer had to herd them. If anything, slowing them down from a miniature stampede taxed his resources. The few minutes between the ridge and the fattening pen gave him time to ponder one final thing.

Christine's pa didn't know she and Slocum were sneaking off whenever they could to enjoy each other's company. Mordecai Magnuson wasn't likely to think well of that since Slocum had overheard him telling his wife how he hoped their daughter would take up with the son of a nearby rancher. Magnuson would turn red as a beet if he ever heard Christine's opinion of young Josh Norton. He would explode like a crate of dynamite if she went on to describe the vile habits Josh Norton's pa, Josh Senior, reputedly enjoyed. Slocum doubted most of it but enjoyed hearing Christine go on about it because it got her hot. And because he got to share in that heat when it turned to passion for him.

For five months they had enjoyed each other in about every way possible, whenever they could, but Slocum was beginning to wonder if a crossroads was coming. After the herd was locked into the cattle cars and rattling along to the slaughterhouses, most of the chores would be over. Magnuson would let go most of the hired help, and that probably included Slocum.

He could simply take his pay. Or he might ask for Christine's hand in marriage. The notion scared him more than it ought to, not because Magnuson might refuse but because Christine might. Being tied down and unable to simply pull up stakes and move on when he felt like it was not something he had thought about much in the past. He was doing that thinking now, and it felt mighty strange.

Strange but right.

Magnuson might never give his permission, but if Christine said yes, that would be it. She'd go with him and never look back, but that left him with only a few months' coin in his pocket and nothing more to support a wife. Eating beans until the cards turned in his favor wouldn't be possible any longer. The responsibility was great.

Christine was worth it.

After the drive, he would ask Christine what she thought about them getting hitched, then worry about her pa. It might be that Slocum read the old man wrong and that he would be happy to see his daughter saddle broke and ridden so both she and Slocum liked it. And it might be that the sun would come up in the west tomorrow.

"Git on in there. Git now!" Slocum used his lariat to shoo the cattle into the feeding pen. He didn't have to invite them twice because of the piles of hay stacked all around and the long tin trough brimming with water.

He closed the gate and sat astride his gelding, watching the cattle gorge themselves. The grasslands were a bit sparse this late in the year because the usual rains had failed more often than they'd come, but he still thought Magnuson had a decent herd that would fetch top dollar.

"Slocum, hey, Slocum! Look what I got!"

He swung around in the saddle and saw the cowboy he'd

taken under his wing come riding up. Slocum blinked, not sure he saw that Tom Garvin actually rode a horse that wasn't a bag of bones. The horse Magnuson had loaned Garvin trotted along behind. The gear on the chestnut was Garvin's, so Slocum reckoned the cowboy had found himself a horse while hunting for strays.

"Ain't this the finest horse you ever did see?"

"Can't say any different," Slocum allowed. "Where'd you find it?"

Garvin's face flowed like molasses in the sun, then firmed up.

"Well, the owner's not gonna miss it none, that's for certain sure."

Garvin launched into the story. As he rambled on, Slocum dismounted and walked his horse to the corral just behind the large barn and began tending the mare. Garvin never slowed down and finally finished in a burst of words that left him huffing and puffing.

"Seems you got as much claim to the horse as anyone does," Slocum said, answering Garvin's unspoken question. "Don't see a brand on its rump." He walked over and examined the horse's teeth, looked in its ears, and then touched the black rope with silver thread running through it.

"Don't!"

Garvin's warning came an instant too late. Slocum's fingers brushed over the rope. He jerked back as if a rattler had bitten him. Sucking his finger, he looked at Garvin questioningly.

"Did the same thing to me," the cowboy said, grinning crookedly. "Can't say why. It was the rope wrapped around the man's neck."

Slocum wasn't superstitious but said, "You might want to get rid of that rope. It's no good."

"Never seen one like it," Garvin said. "I'm gonna keep it."

Slocum shrugged it off.

"Slocum! Get your ass over here. I got an errand for you!"

"The boss is calling me," Slocum said. He gave the chestnut one last pat on the neck. "You take good care of this one. She's a keeper."

"I will, Slocum, I will!" Garvin beamed.

Slocum hurried to the ranch house back door, where Magnuson stood impatiently.

"You took your sweet time."

"What can I do for you?"

Magnuson glowered, then said, "I got a long list of supplies for the missus to get picked up in town. Get a wagon hitched up and fetch it back pronto." He thrust out a sheet of paper with long columns of what needed to be bought, written in a neat hand. To himself, he muttered, "May as well buy the whole damn store."

Slocum took the list and folded it up.

"Be back by sundown. We got to finish finding the strays, and I want all hands on the range early in the morning."

It was only ten miles into Central City. Slocum knew it would be well past sundown when he returned, no matter how recklessly he drove getting to town. Return had to be slower since the wagon would be heavily loaded.

"Papa, I need some cloth."

Slocum perked up. The voice from in the house came as music to his ears. Christine Magnuson stepped out and hung on her father's arm, looking up at him with her dancing blue eyes.

"He can get it for you. Tell him what you need."

"Him?" Christine sounded scornful. As she looked at Slocum, she gave him a broad wink. "He'd as like bring back a gunny sack. Besides, I need to decide. You know this is for Mama's curtains."

"For her birthday," Magnuson said, looking glum. He fixed Slocum with a gimlet eye. "You look after her, you hear?"

"Yes, sir," Slocum said. "I'll get the team hitched."

Slocum tried not to run when he went to the barn to get

the team and hitch up the two horses to the wagon. With a light jump, he was in the driver's box, reins in hand. He snapped them and got the team pulling. This was turning into everyone's lucky day. Garvin had found himself a horse worth riding, and now Slocum was sent on an otherwise boring trip to pick up supplies with the sexiest woman within fifty miles.

"Up you go. You put all that curtain . . . stuff on the ranch account," Magnuson said to his daughter. He held her easily, his large hands around her slender waist. Then he set her lightly into the box alongside Slocum. "Don't drive too fast," Magnuson cautioned.

"No, sir, won't." Slocum snapped the reins, and the team pulled hard, causing Christine to grab his arm to keep from being tossed into the empty bed. He heard Magnuson cursing behind him and then they were far enough away that it no longer mattered what the rancher said.

"That's mighty bold of you, John Slocum," she said.

"What's that?"

"Almost tossing me back like that so I had to grab on to your strong arm for support." Christine took his arm and rested her head against his shoulder.

"You going to do that all the way into town?" he asked. "Not that I'm complaining, mind you, but the road's mighty rough in places."

"Oh, spoilsport," she said, sitting upright. But she didn't move away. Her leg pressed warmly into his.

They rode into town like this, talking of nothing in particular, but Slocum was always aware of the woman and how she moved back and forth against him, even when the motion of the wagon bouncing along didn't require it. She was a sexy kitten, purring and stroking him.

Central City sat in a bowl, surrounded by low hills. Slocum kept the team moving at a steady pace but knew the return would be more difficult, a good portion uphill, and with a loaded wagon, the horses would have their work cut out for them.

He pulled back on the reins and stomped on the brake in front of the general store. Before he could lash the reins around the brake handle and help Christine down, she jumped lightly to the street and ran around the wagon, going up the three creaking wood steps to the front porch of the store. In the wink of an eye she vanished inside. Slocum took his time getting down. He pulled out the list and eyed it. Magnuson hadn't been joking when he said his missus had ordered damned near everything in the store.

"Afternoon," he said, tipping his hat to the owner's wife. She hardly acknowledged him, being too busy showing Christine bolt after bolt of cloth. Slocum was no judge but most of it didn't appear to be good for making curtains. Dresses, maybe, but not curtains. He hesitated when he saw how Christine ran her fingers over some white lace. Was she thinking the same thing he had earlier?

"What'll it be, Slocum?" The owner came over and took the list from his hands. "You fixin' to hole up for the rest of the year? Never mind. Mr. Magnuson always was a belt and suspenders sort. Give me a hand getting it out to the wagon."

For the next half hour Slocum worked alongside the merchant, putting sugar, flour, grain, and a host of other supplies into the wagon bed.

"And the bolt of cloth, too," the storekeeper said, brushing his hands off on his apron.

Slocum hurried to help Christine awkwardly wrestle the cloth into the back of the wagon.

"Thank you," she said. Her hand lingered a moment on his, then she hastily pulled it away before the store owner noticed. "Is everything loaded, Mr. Slocum?"

He nodded. The storekeeper had already gone back into the mercantile, busily tending two women who had come in with lists of their own.

"We should get back to the ranch," Slocum said. "It'll be an hour or more longer on the return trip."

"Yes, of course, the weight," Christine said, eyeing the load. Slocum and the storekeeper had laid it down from side to side. She walked around and waited for him to help her up onto the hard wooden seat.

"You want to get something to eat? I don't think your pa would object."

"Let's not and say we did," she told him, grinning broadly.

He headed out of town, up the slope of the rim of the bowl where the town rested and then vanished from sight. The road was straight and empty as far as the eye could see.

"Not many travelers today," Christine said. She leaned back, unfurled the cloth she had bought, and stretched it out over the sacks of flour and sugar.

"Not anyone I can see," Slocum said.

She threw her hands up in the air and tumbled back into the wagon bed.

"Oh, that's harder than I thought."

"But not harder than the loft in the barn."

"Not as hard," she agreed. "We started there with hay under us but we were too . . . active." Christine reached up and began unbuttoning her blouse. Slocum watched the slow revelation of twin globes of snowy flesh slip out. She cupped them and bounced them a little, then pinched her own nipples until they were hard and red with arousal.

"Oh, yes," she said, closing her eyes and moaning. "That feels so good. But it would feel better if a *man* was doing it."

Slocum hit a pothole and sent her sitting back, her arms supporting her body. With her legs stretched in front of her, Christine slowly raised her knees. The wind caught her skirt and lifted it to reveal shapely legs—and even more.

"No, I'm not wearing anything else," she said in a husky voice. "Just for you, John. Just for you." She rocked back and hoisted her feet to the back of the seat, causing her skirt to slip down and reveal her naked privates.

Slocum worked to fasten the reins to either side of the seat. He had driven nails under the board seat for just such a chance at letting the horses continue on their way back to the ranch on their own without him driving them. Both leather straps were secured. He made sure the horses weren't spooked and kept a steady, slow pace. The gait was not what Slocum would have chosen for them—it was slower.

And that suited him just fine.

He swung around, got his boots into the wagon bed, Christine's feet on either side of his hips. He dropped to his knees and pitched forward, bearing her flat onto her back.

"Oh, John, you're not going to take advantage of poor li'l ole me?"

"I certainly intend to," he said. Then he quieted her joking with a deep, hard kiss.

She threw her arms around his neck and pulled him down even harder. Their lips parted and their tongues began dancing about, teasing and toying, moving back and forth until both were panting from their rising desire. Slocum moved from the woman's ruby lips to her slender throat and into the deep valley between her luscious breasts. The mounds of female flesh jiggled as the wagon rattled along. Slocum caught one nipple and suckled a moment, released it, and went to the other. Christine writhed about under him.

Then her legs wrapped around his waist and pulled him down into her crotch.

"Oh!"

Slocum knew this wasn't going to work without some accommodation. He unfastened his gun belt and cast it aside, but he had help working on the buttons holding his fly shut. Her fingers fumbled about, popping open the buttons one by one until he leaped out, long and hard and ready.

"Oh, yes," she said breathlessly. Her knees rose higher as she pulled him forward, down to her bush, and then, with a rush, all the way into her moist, hot core.

Suddenly surrounded, Slocum stopped all movement and

simply relished the clutching heat all around his manhood. The rocking motion of the wagon, the occasion bump, the unexpected surges as the horses changed gait all moved his steely shaft about within her.

Christine clung to him fiercely and began rolling her hips around to take him even deeper within. The triple movements—hers, his, and the wagon's—all pushed them higher until they ached for release.

Slocum felt the fiery tide building in his balls but held back. It was a long way back to the ranch, and he wanted to make this last as long as possible.

"I . . . I need you, John," Christine gasped out. She half climbed up him, her arms around his neck and her hips thrusting back and forth.

The motion proved impossible to deny. Slocum began thrusting to meet her movement and soon they fell into the age-old rhythm of a man loving a woman. He cried out when he could no longer hold back and spilled his seed within her. But she didn't hear. She was sobbing out her own climax.

Locked together, they clung to each other for long minutes, then sank down to the rude bed formed by the sacks of sugar and flour.

"That was over too quick," Slocum said.

"Disappointed?"

"Hardly. Not ever with you, but there should have been more."

Christine laughed and said, "You're so greedy, John. But I agree. I'm greedy, too. And still horny!"

She pushed away from him and swung about so she could thrust her head between his legs. She took his limp worm into her mouth and began working on it. With her own pubes just inches from his face, Slocum craned his neck a mite and started licking and kissing the exposed flesh. Christine trembled at this avid tongue-lashing. And he hardened even more as she sucked harder on him.

They'd barely finished this time before the team reached

the edge of the Bar M Ranch. Slocum hoped the look on his face and the flush to Christine's cheeks didn't arouse any suspicion, but the twilight saved them from being discovered.

Magnuson bellowed for his daughter to get into the house for dinner and for Slocum to unload the wagon.

With every sack Slocum moved to the storage, he remembered what he and Christine had done atop it on the way back. Somehow, that made the chore go faster and every sack seem a bit lighter.

3

Slocum leaned on the corral fence watching the foreman work a mustang brought in from the range. The piebald horse was a mean one, kicking and bucking and doing everything Slocum had ever seen to keep from being saddled and broken. He had to jump back when the horse got away from Jed Blassingame, amid a stream of cursing volatile enough to turn the air blue.

"Fer the love of God, Jed, keep that danged animal from kickin' the living hell out of us," complained a cowboy who'd climbed up on the corral and sat with his legs dangling over.

"Keep yer own danged body away or I'll be the one doin' the kickin'," Blassingame yelled. "And it'll be yer damned ass that I kick!" He stomped over to where the horse faced him, eyes wide and nostrils flaring. Slocum couldn't tell which showed the most fire and determination. The foreman wasn't a man to give up, but he had to admit it looked as if Blassingame might have met his match in the mustang.

"He's having a time of it, ain't he?"

Slocum looked over his shoulder. Tom Garvin strutted up, swinging his fancy black rope with the silver strands in

18

it. For a greenhorn, he did a good job of keeping a loop. He even gave the feeling of having such confidence that he could do that from horseback to lasso a calf and bring it down for proper branding. Slocum had to wonder at the change in the young man since he had found the body out on the range.

"Hard one to break," Slocum said. "I've seen outlaws tougher in my day, but not many. And not ones inclined to think about how they're going to be mean." Slocum rested his chin on his crossed arms along the top corral rail and watched. The horse was mad and scared, but the intelligence in the eyes told of willingness to do whatever was necessary to outwit a cowboy trying to break it so it could get back with its herd.

"Is Jed gonna saddle it up and break it that way?"

"Got to get a rope halter on first. Maybe calm the horse then, press it against a rail, and see what needs to be done. I'm mighty glad that's not my job."

"You afraid of that horse, Slocum? Never thought I'd hear you say such a thing." Garvin laughed. Slocum looked hard at him. The young cowboy was mocking him, ridiculing him. He wouldn't go so far as to say he was calling him out, but he skirted mighty close to that.

Even worse, the other cowboys watching their foreman work the horse overheard and were intent on the exchange. Slocum had tried to keep a low profile, especially since he didn't want it becoming gossip how he and Christine were getting on. So far as he could tell, nobody, even Garvin, had a hint of suspicion about him and the rancher's daughter. If that happened, he wasn't quite sure what he would do. Drift on, in all likelihood, but the thought of settling down with a filly as lovely and frisky as Christine Magnuson wormed its way into his brain. He wasn't looking to cash in on her daddy's ranch—that notion made Slocum even antsier about the cowboys finding out.

He wasn't the kind to live off another man's hard-won

riches, and the Bar M was a fine ranch. Slocum would be happier starting on his own and building off that.

He shook himself. Every time he thought of Christine, he began making plans. That wasn't anything he had done in a very long time—since before the war. His brother, Robert, had been the hunter and was older by a couple years. He would have inherited Slocum's Stand in Calhoun, Georgia. That didn't bother Slocum overmuch. If anything, Robert might have decided to move on, leaving the farm to Slocum, who had always been a better farmer.

But the war had changed everything. Robert had been killed during Pickett's ill-fated charge. Slocum touched his watch pocket and the timepiece resting there. This was the only legacy he had from his brother or anyone else in the family. He had tangled with William Quantrill, gotten gut-shot and left for dead. Long months of painful recovery had passed before he had been able to return to Georgia, where he found that his parents had both died sometime earlier. The farm ought to have been his by law, but a carpetbagger judge had taken a fancy to the spread.

He wanted the land to raise Tennessee walkers and had trumped up fake bills that showed no taxes had been paid during the war years. When he and a hired gunman had ridden out to seize the property, Slocum had left. And behind him were two fresh graves down by the spring house. He had traveled west, dogged by wanted posters for killing a federal judge. Even crooked, Yankee judges mattered to the law.

But not since he had ridden off, the Georgia sun warm on his back as he headed westward, had Slocum seriously considered settling down. That arrest warrant might be a problem, but he hadn't come across a bounty hunter looking for him in a year or more. It wasn't forgotten because judge killing was a crime, no matter what kind of snake in the grass the judge was, but if he settled down and proved some land and became an upstanding citizen, nobody around might much care what a bounty hunter or federal lawman thought.

"What's wrong, Slocum? You got a far-off look in your eye. Ain't never seen you lookin' like that before."

"Nothing," he said, turning from Garvin. It never paid to wear your heart on your sleeve or let others, especially casual acquaintances, know what was going on in your head.

Still, settling down might not be such a bad thing.

He jumped when the piebald kicked out and struck the rail just under his hands.

"You kin break it, Slocum. You got the look of a real bronc buster 'bout you," called Blassingame.

"You just don't want to do it yourself," Slocum said. He considered the horse and how it sunfished when it left the ground, belly going toward the sky as it arched its back. It was a mean one, but he might be able to do some good. "What's it worth?"

"A dollar," Blassingame said without hesitation, telling Slocum the man would go higher. He did. He agreed to five dollars if Slocum rode the mustang until it got all tuckered out.

From the power in the horse's legs, that might be quite a while, but Slocum wasn't any tyro. In his day he had broken worse.

"You gonna do it, Slocum?" Garvin asked, almost out of breath. He had a wild look in his eye, as if he needed some breaking, too.

"Bring that cayuse by the rail," Slocum said. "I'll get him saddle broke or know the reason."

Blassingame and two others forced the piebald to the rail. The four of them got a saddle screwed down tight. As the three cowboys threw their shoulders against the horse, it took a side step and gave Slocum the chance to climb into the saddle by stepping off the corral fence.

For a moment, the piebald simply stood. Slocum thought he was going to earn the easiest five dollars ever. Might have been that the horse had been broken but lit out and joined the wild herd and was remembering what it meant to have a rider astride its back.

Then the horse unwound like a powerful spring. Slocum didn't know how the piebald could launch straight into the air without any buildup, but it did. He was caught by surprise and went sailing through the air, to land hard in the dirt. Rolling to his hands and knees, he found himself almost eye to eye with the horse.

"I swear, that nag's laughin' at you, Slocum," Tom Garvin said. This produced a round of real laughter from the other hands.

Slocum got mad, as much at letting down his guard the way he had as at the truth in Garvin's words. The horse *was* laughing at him the only way it could.

Getting to his feet, he dusted himself off and said, "I'll try once more."

"I'll only give you four bucks now," Blassingame said, "since the horse's already given you one!"

This caused a new round of laughter from the cowboys. Slocum ignored them and stared hard at the horse, who accepted his challenge by letting him step up into the saddle without so much as a quiver. When horse and rider went airborne this time, Slocum was ready. He clung to the saddle horn with one hand and the bridle with the other, determined not to sail like a bird again.

He barely clung to the horse as it hung suspended midair, then landed with enough of a jolt to crack Slocum's teeth. His head snapped back, and he felt himself sliding to one side. Slocum was ready for this and bent low, his knees pressing in as hard as he could. This produced a new attempt to dislodge him. The piebald spun in a tight circle, then reversed on a dime and gave him some change.

Dizzy from the spinning, Slocum was no match for another rocketing into the air. The horse bent almost double as if it could shove its belly up through its back. When they landed, Slocum went tumbling over the horse's head, hit the ground hard, and lay flat on his back. The breath had been knocked out of his lungs.

Blassingame and the other cowboys were slow in going to his aid when the piebald decided to end the matter with a heavy hoof in the middle of his chest. Slocum saw the unshod hoof descending but couldn't find the strength to dodge.

And then a cheer went up. Slocum gasped, sat up, and looked behind him. Tom Garvin had swung his fancy black lariat and roped the piebald's front hoof. How he had tugged hard enough to unbalance the horse was a mystery, but it saved Slocum's life. The horse hobbled about, front leg secured by the loop of rope.

"Git on outta here, Slocum. You're done for the day," the foreman said. Blassingame helped Slocum up, but there wasn't any need for the support. Slocum left the corral on his own, seething at how the horse had outwitted him again.

"That's a devil horse, I swear," Blassingame said. "You was doin' just fine and then it got you with the slickest moves I ever did see."

"Thanks," Slocum said, slapping Garvin on the back and ignoring the foreman. "You saved me out there."

"Shucks, wasn't nuthin'," Garvin said. He pushed past Slocum and faced Blassingame. "Let me try."

"Try what?" The foreman stared at the tenderfoot with a puzzled look on his leathery face.

"Breakin' that animal."

"Slocum couldn't do it. Why do you want to get yourself kilt?"

"I kin do it," Garvin said doggedly. "I will."

"You saved my hide out there," Slocum said. "Let me return the favor. Don't even try. That one's smart, fast, strong, and worse, he's a killer. Your best bet's to let it go."

"Five dollars?" Garvin pressed. "You said you'd give Slocum five dollars."

"Ten for you," Blassingame said.

Slocum bristled. The foreman was egging on a man who didn't have a ghost of an idea what he was in for.

"You might as well lasso a tornado and try to ride it. Forget it, Tom. Nobody'll think less of you for not trying— but they will if you're too dumb to know you'll get yourself killed."

"Ten?"

Slocum saw that the foreman held sway over Garvin, and he and the rest wanted some more entertainment. That it might come with a man's death didn't bother them one whit. He stepped back to let Garvin learn his lesson—if he survived.

Slocum refused to help get the piebald into position again. Garvin snapped his fancy black rope off the horse's leg. He swung it in a perfect loop and dropped it around the horse's neck. The piebald settled down rather than strangle itself, obviously knowing what was to follow. It had patience enough to bide its time and unseat a new fool trying to ride it.

"Watch me, Slocum. See how it's done!" Tom Garvin settled down, got his feet into the stirrups, and then was launched so high Slocum wondered if he would ever come down. During the war he had heard stories of cannonballs fired so high they vanished for all time, and for a few seconds he thought Garvin would find what had happened to them.

Then the tenderfoot crashed to the ground so hard it actually shook like an earthquake. Slocum was reaching for his six-gun to shoot the horse if it tried to stomp Garvin the way it had him, but the horse whinnied and trotted to the far side of the corral, secure and smug in yet another victory over a damn fool rider.

"Tarnation, get him outta there," bellowed the foreman. "Don't want him stomped to death."

Slocum vaulted over the railing and dropped to the

ground, wary of the horse. The piebald pawed the dirt like a bull ready to charge.

He considered dragging out his iron again and putting them all out of the misery caused by the horse, but the animal's instincts for survival were strong enough to scent the pure hatred boiling from Slocum. The horse backed away and let him get his hands under Garvin's shoulder. He dragged the cowboy from the arena, his spurs cutting deep furrows in the dirt.

"He still alive?" Blassingame peered over at Garvin but didn't approach to find out for certain. He left that chore to Slocum.

"Far as I can tell, he's in one piece." Slocum checked arms and legs and Garvin didn't wince. The man's breathing was thready and shallow, and when Slocum pried open his eyelids, he saw that the pupils were different sizes. "Seen this before. He might be all right, but he has to be kept moving."

"We got work to do," Blassingame said. "You tend him, whatever it takes to keep him from dyin', but don't dawdle."

Slocum shot him a cold look. The foreman had never caught Slocum trying to get out of doing his fair share and wasn't likely to now.

"He ain't as important as rounding up the strays. We got a herd to move to the rail yard next week, and every one of them damned beeves is worth more than his salary."

Slocum heaved, got Garvin to his feet, then put a shoulder under him. The added weight from the slight cowboy was hardly noticed as Slocum made his way to the bunkhouse. He kicked open the door with a loud bang, not noticing he had broken a board. With a quick turn, he put Garvin into a chair at the rickety table where they played five-card stud every night.

"You come on," Slocum urged, holding a tin cup with tepid water to the man's lips. Garvin stirred but didn't do more than moan in response. Slocum dashed the water in his face. This got the dazed man's attention.

"Wha—" Garvin stirred and his eyelids fluttered. "Whassit? Rainin'?"

"On your feet and walk." Slocum dragged him up, got his arm around his shoulder, and started Garvin putting one foot ahead of the other until they reached the far wall of the bunkhouse. Then they retraced their steps. Garvin was stronger by the time they made their third trip.

"You keep walking on your own. Do it," Slocum ordered.

"Wanna sit down."

"Walk." Slocum's tone brooked no challenge. Garvin walked.

"What happened? Don't rightly remember much. The horse . . ."

"He threw you even higher 'n he did me," Slocum said. "That outlaw's no good. Blassingame ought to either let it go or have Hashknife make us up some special steaks for supper."

"I'm getting some of it back now. I was doin' jist fine and then I was sailin' through the air." Garvin made slapping motions, then looked around in a panic. "Where's my rope?"

Slocum shook his head. He hadn't paid a whole lot of attention to such things, not with the spill Garvin had taken.

"He stole it! That mangy son of a buck stole it!"

"What are you going on about?"

Garvin fixed hard eyes on Slocum. Any hint of having his brains scrambled was gone—or maybe not.

"Blassingame. He wanted my rope. He cain't steal it!"

"Settle down. You—" Slocum was talking to empty air. Garvin had bulled his way out of the bunkhouse, slamming the door behind him so hard the board Slocum had broken came free and clattered to the floor.

Heaving himself to his feet, Slocum followed. Garvin was still feeling the effects of smashing his head into the

ground. Which was harder, head or dirt, was a matter that'd
have to be settled, and Garvin ought to do it after he had
slept on it a spell now that the concussion was a thing of the
past.

Slocum reached the corral in time to see scrawny Tom
Garvin shove Blassingame so hard that the foreman stumbled and fell onto his ass.

"You stole it. Admit it. You wanted my rope!" Garvin
stood over the fallen man, hands clenched into puny fists. It
would have been funny if both men hadn't looked so
serious.

So deadly serious.

The foreman was fuming mad, and Garvin had passed
the point where simple persuasion would work.

"Don't," Slocum warned. "He's not got a gun strapped
on." His own hand touched the ebony butt of his Colt. Blassingame was within a heartbeat of throwing down on Garvin.

"He stole my rope. He can't just take it. He won't. I won't
damned let him!"

"Settle down," Slocum said, stepping between Garvin
and the foreman. To his surprise, Tom Garvin turned on
him. The punch he delivered wouldn't have been noticed
except Slocum hadn't expected it. He took a step back and
his feet tangled with Blassingame's. He sat down heavily
and stared in amazement at the young cowboy. The change
in him was like night and day. Normally peaceable enough
and eager as a puppy dog, the other Garvin was a pleasant
enough trail companion.

Slocum had stepped on rattlers that were more accommodating than this Tom Garvin.

"You in this, too, Slocum? You and him tryin' to steal
my rope?"

"You're not in your right mind. Settle down, Tom.
Nobody's out to take your rope."

"I want it."

Slocum had heard that tone of voice before and seen the set to men's bodies just before they went into a killing rage. Garvin was pulling on a homicidal rage before his eyes.

"It's back there. In the corral," Blassingame said, sitting up.

"Ain't nobody want that worthless hunk of hemp. Don't even bend right, not with that silver stripe in it."

"He's right," Slocum said, pointing. "There on the top rail. Your rope."

Garvin panted harshly, took a quick look, and then stomped over and snatched the rope as if it might grow wings and fly away.

"Satisfied?" Slocum asked, getting to his feet.

Garvin was panting harshly, as if he had run a long race. His head bobbed up and down. Slocum doubted he could answer any other way.

"I sure as hell ain't satisfied," Blassingame said, climbing to his feet. "You get yer gear—and that includes that damned rope—and clear out. You're fired, Garvin, and if I see your worthless hide on Bar M land, I'll do more than fire your ass!"

"You're going to be a man short for the trail drive," Slocum said. He didn't owe Garvin anything, but he felt sorry for him. When a man lost everything, he clung to what little came his way. As far as he could tell, there wasn't anything left for Garvin if he got fired from the Bar M.

Blassingame scowled at Slocum. The meaning was clear as the azure blue sky domed over their heads. If Slocum pushed the issue any more, he'd be riding off the Bar M spread, too.

A hundred things raced through Slocum's head. Garvin was unreasonable, but he wasn't thinking straight because of the knock to his head. Blassingame could be more accommodating. In another circumstance, he would have ridden off with Garvin, but not now.

Christine.

He wasn't going to give her up over a crazy cowboy's love affair with a length of black rope.

"You got fifteen minutes to get outta my sight." Blassingame turned to Slocum. "What's it gonna be?"

Slocum looked at a still furious Tom Garvin, then said to Blassingame, "That box canyon to the south might have a few strays. I'll see how many I can find there."

Blassingame stormed off, muttering to himself. Slocum started to talk to Garvin and maybe convince him to apologize and get his job back. He had gone, too, dragging his black rope so that it left a trail like a sidewinder's in the dirt.

4

Slocum rode alongside the foreman, keeping his thoughts to himself. Garvin wasn't such a bad kid. He was ignorant, but he could learn. What Slocum hadn't counted on was him being stupid, too. Nothing would cure him of that until he had taken enough hard wallops to knock some sense into his thick head. Something about him and the rope made for a bad combination, though Slocum had been amazed at some of the good luck Garvin had. When he had taken a header off the piebald, he had smashed straight down onto the hard ground. A fall like that should have killed him outright or at least broken his neck. All he had suffered was a bit of a concussion, and that wasn't too severe. Slocum had walked him until the worst of the effect passed.

But tangling with Blassingame over the rope the way he had went past stupid. The foreman didn't suffer fools lightly and was as like to have beaten Garvin to a bloody pulp as fire him for what he said. Slocum tried to put that arrogance Garvin had shown off to the fall that had cracked his skull, but there hadn't been any other evidence of having his senses addled.

Slocum pushed it out of his mind. He didn't need to be wet-nursing a man like Tom Garvin. He was old enough to look after himself, even if that meant getting into fights with men likely to knock his block off. Still, Slocum had to count the young cowboy as having another bit of good luck. Blassingame *hadn't* hauled off and decked him.

"You figure some strays went down that canyon?"

Slocum looked at the foreman. Blassingame had been mighty quiet on their ride away from the Bar M ranch house, too. What he had worked over in his head didn't show on his face. Slocum knew better than to ask.

"Water there? I see where a dry creek bed meanders on back."

"The spring feeding the creek might have dried up, but maybe a pool's enough to get them stupid varmints to leave the stock ponds for it."

They both turned their horses' faces and rode into the high-walled canyon. Slocum looked around, growing uneasy as they went deeper into it.

"Ain't Injuns around these parts right now. All of 'em on the rez are staying put."

Slocum kept looking to the high rims. To reach either side would require a considerable amount of riding. The trails leading up looked chancy at best.

"You're gettin' as jumpy as a long-tailed cat flopped near a rocker," Blassingame said. "You don't like tight spaces?"

"It's not that," Slocum said. He couldn't put his finger on what made him uneasy. "There any other way out of the canyon?"

"Well, can't rightly say. There are box canyons all over this area, but I've never rid into this one to find out. You worryin' them beeves have snuck out the other end?"

"That's it," Slocum said, hoping the lie didn't sound like one. He wished Blassingame had scouted this terrain before and knew something about it. The walls begged for Indians to shove boulders onto their heads or even have a sharpshooter or two take potshots at them. Why he thought that worried him even more. He had gotten through the war by listening to this sixth sense. It was prodding him a mite now, but he felt sharper pokes building.

"Fresh cow flop? See it? Hell, I can smell it."

They rode over and chased off a swarm of flies. Slocum saw the cattle hoofprints in the softer earth.

"Might be a half dozen," he said. "Maybe more." He frowned, then turned his horse for the far wall.

"What you find?"

Slocum dismounted and studied the rocky ground. Some rocks had bright silver streaks showing something shod had ridden this way. A horse, probably with a rider. But he couldn't tell how long ago it had been. Maybe the cattle came afterward or the rider was lost. Try as he might, he couldn't tell which way the rider had traveled. Might have been from the canyon rather than into it.

"Don't see no sign of them beeves comin' out. We can round 'em up and be back for Hashknife to poison us with more of that slop he calls stew."

"The biscuits aren't bad," Slocum said, but he wasn't thinking of the cook's ineptness or the odd things he tossed into the stewpot and called it "kwee-zine like them Frenchies eat."

"Not bad? He makes 'em using cement. And the gravy he pours over 'em—what's that?" Blassingame drew rein and cocked his head to one side, listening to the commotion from the far end of the canyon.

"Horses," Slocum said. "Riders rounding up cattle."

"Ain't nobody else from the ranch came this way. That means rustlers." Blassingame didn't wear a sidearm. He pulled his rifle from the saddle scabbard and fumbled in his saddlebags to find a box of cartridges. Methodically stuffing the rounds into the magazine took only a few seconds. He looked up at Slocum. "You up to chasin' 'em off?"

Slocum touched the butt of his Colt Navy and nodded.

"We kin wait for 'em to drive the cattle to us and catch 'em in a crossfire. Or we kin go after 'em." From the way Blassingame spoke, he preferred the latter since he wasn't much when it came to patience.

Slocum looked up at the canyon rim again, squinting as he studied the westernmost side. Shielding his eyes with his hand, he thought he caught sight of a glint off something silver.

"We go to them," Slocum said, mounting. "They got lookouts posted above us."

"What? Where?"

"Unless they are damned good marksmen, they'll never hit us, but they can warn the others we're on the way."

"Let 'em set a trap. We know they're ahead of us!"

Slocum didn't bother pointing out they had no idea if they went after two rustlers or a dozen. If the gang was big enough that they could spare at least one lookout along the rim, the fight they were willing to give as strangers rode into the canyon might be a nasty one.

"What do you think, Slocum? Charge right on in?"

"They know we're coming, but we don't know anything about them," he answered in a low voice. He was aware of how sounds were magnified in this stretch of canyon, where the walls squeezed down even more. The lowing of cattle from ahead drowned out any sounds of riders, though he thought he heard an occasional snap of a rope or bullwhip as the cattle were being rounded up.

"That won't slow me none. You ain't thinkin' on lettin' Mr. Magnuson down, now are you, Slocum?"

"Not looking to get killed for any man," Slocum said. As Blassingame bristled, he went on. "Let me scout some before we bull our way into what might be a shooting gallery—with us as the sitting ducks."

"Don't take long. I got a bad feelin' that this here canyon ain't a box, and they might be stealin' the cows from under our noses."

Slocum took a long look at the rim, knowing their presence had already been passed on to the rustlers on the canyon floor. He rode to the sheer rock wall and pressed close. This would keep the man above him from dropping rocks or even getting a decent shot off. Advancing slowly, he heard men yelling now and frightened cattle getting even more agitated at being moved.

He wanted to gallop ahead to see what was happening, but his words to Blassingame kept him cautious. Rounding a turn in the canyon opened a vista to him that caused his gut to turn into a giant knot. A half-dozen men circled the small herd of twenty beeves. Magnuson wouldn't take kindly to losing that many head of cattle, but Slocum wasn't looking too kindly on trying to stop the rustlers either. Two used whips to drive the cattle while the other four worked as outriders, chasing down any steer clever enough to get away from the herd.

They worked their stolen cattle toward the far end of the canyon. From all Slocum could tell, this was a box canyon, but they had something in mind. He blinked when he saw two more riders appear as if from thin air. He knew then that a rock wall hid the exit from the canyon. Turning his horse, he started back to warn Blassingame when gunfire erupted. At the bottom of the canyon, he thought the gunshots came from every direction. Echoes rattled from side to side and confused him whether they came from behind or ahead.

Worse, they might be coming from snipers up along the far canyon rim. If they did, he wouldn't have a chance.

He put his head down and trotted through the tumble of rocks, making as good a speed as he could without risking his horse breaking a leg. He discarded even this when a bullet spanged off the rock wall above his head and showered him with hot shards.

"Too many of them," he called out to Blassingame. The

foreman had his rifle out, swinging it all around but not finding a target.

"Where are them varmints?" Bullets tore past him, making him even more frantic. Blassingame started firing. He was more dangerous to Slocum in that instant than to the rustlers.

"Get your head down, dammit," Slocum shouted. "We either try to make a stand or we run for it."

"I ain't runnin'! I was hired—"

A bullet jerked at Blassingame's right arm and pulled away some of his duster. Red began to stain the canvas as he reached over with his left hand and swatted at the wound as if it were nothing more than an annoying mosquito.

Slocum reached the foreman and shoved him hard enough to unseat him. He landed hard, his rifle pinned under his body.

"What you doin', boy? You cain't—"

Dust rose in tiny spires all around. He finally realized the danger they were in.

"Up on the rims. Both rims," Slocum said. He hit the ground and grabbed for his Winchester in its saddle sheath. A handgun wouldn't do him any good at this range.

"How many of them?" Blassingame finally got his wits about him. He had turned pale and trembled. Slocum couldn't tell if it was from the wound or the man's courage was running out along with his life's blood.

"More 'n we can handle," Slocum said. He rested his rifle on a rock, took careful aim, adjusted for firing uphill, then squeezed off a shot. He missed the rifleman on the rim by a foot, but it was close enough to drive the man back undercover.

"We kin fight 'em off. Me and you kin do it, Slocum."

Slocum turned his rifle to the half-dozen rustlers riding from the depths of the canyon. He emptied his magazine without bringing down a single outlaw.

"You got more ammo?"

"In my saddlebags." Blassingame looked around and saw his and Slocum's horses had run a few yards away. He heaved himself to his feet and lumbered toward his horse. He grunted as another bullet came close to ending his life. The foreman dug in his saddlebags and got the box of cartridges. With a backhand toss, he heaved them in Slocum's direction, then simply sat down hard.

The box tumbled through the air, spewing out its brass cartridges until only a few were left inside when Slocum grabbed it. Quickly reloading, he fired a few times to keep the advancing rustlers honest, then bent low and scooped up as many shells as he could getting to Blassingame's side.

"You hurt bad?"

"Feelin' kinda woozy. Legs don't seem to want to hold me up."

Slocum ripped open the duster and saw Blassingame had been hit twice. The first wound was the worst, going through his arm and then into his chest. He probed a mite, Blassingame let out a howl of pain, then Slocum pulled his hand back, wiping the blood onto the man's duster.

"Not as bad as it might have been. The bullet broke a rib but didn't puncture your hide more 'n a shallow scratch."

"Breathin' is a chore," Blassingame said. "Reminds me when I busted myself up gettin' kicked by a milk cow when I was nine years old. Pa tole me not to get behind the cow. She was a mean one, she was." He winced as Slocum tore away part of the foreman's shirt. The other wound was shallow. He could see the butt end of the bullet still sticking out. It had been almost spent by the time it hit the foreman.

With bullets filling the air around them, Slocum concentrated only on the wound. He used Blassingame's own knife to cut out the bullet.

"That gonna fix me up?" The foreman winced as Slocum pressed his torn, bloody shirt down onto the wound.

"Only worry you'll have is cleaning your knife blade,"

Slocum assured him. He scooped up Blassingame's rifle, emptied it in the direction of the approaching rustlers, and then pulled his own back to his shoulder.

The outlaws took cover, giving Slocum some hope that he had at least winged one of them. If he could keep them wary enough, he and Blassingame might get away alive.

"Why don't they see to their rustlin' and jist let us go?" Blassingame had turned pale under his weathered hide. "Cain't think we're the law. Not out here."

"They might not want us to fetch the law." It would be weeks, if ever, before the cattle were missed. Even then, Magnuson might not be too worried about finding them. Wolves and coyotes took a meal or two from any herd. This year it might be that hungrier wolves had moved down from the hills because it had been drier than normal.

If the rustlers killed him and Blassingame, there'd be no witnesses to their crime, and they'd have some mighty fine eating when they got around to celebrating the theft. From what Slocum had heard, ranchers adjoining the Bar M weren't inclined to pay much attention to brands. The outlaws need only find one such rancher and they could ride away with their pockets stuffed with greenbacks.

"White flag," Blassingame said. "We can parley with them."

Slocum knew that wasn't likely. The outlaws held all the aces. They had the cattle, they had the numerical superiority, and worst of all, they had all the time in the world to eliminate witnesses.

"Can you ride? I'll draw them away, then you ride like the demons of hell are on your tail. Get back to the ranch and send help."

"Run off? I ain't a coward."

"You'll be the hero, bringing back the rest of the hands to save the herd."

Slocum realized how badly Blassingame had been injured when this made sense to the foreman.

"There won't be much time. They're moving on us." Slocum couldn't see the outlaws but suspected they were trying to circle and catch them from three sides, letting the gunmen on the rim take care of any possible retreat.

"I kin ride," Blassingame said. He tried to stand, sat heavily, then grabbed Slocum's arm. "Help me up, will you, Slocum?"

With a heave, Slocum got him to his feet. To his credit, Blassingame mounted under his own power, then slumped forward. Slocum wished there was time to lash the man into the saddle. The shouts from both flanks convinced him that wasn't going to happen.

For a moment he considered riding with Blassingame. The man was on the verge of blacking out, and if he did, neither of them would get away. The rustlers were closing in fast, and giving them his back as a target didn't set well with Slocum. Then this route to safety disappeared. A stray bullet caught Slocum's horse in the center of its forehead. The mare collapsed as if all the bones in its legs had turned to mush. He cursed the loss, then knew he could lose far more than a good mount.

He slapped the rump of Blassingame's horse. The foreman was almost unseated as it rocketed from the canyon. Slocum twisted about and got off three fast shots at the rifleman stationed on the canyon rim trying to sight in on the foreman. His shots went wide of their mark, but again he drove the sniper back, giving Blassingame a chance. Not much of one, but a chance.

Slocum turned to keep the two rustlers on his left at bay, only to find he came up empty. Using his six-shooter, he gained himself a few seconds to hunt for the shining brass casings in the dry canyon bottom. He rolled behind a boulder and stuffed in the four rounds he had retrieved. A quick look around didn't reveal any others.

"We got 'im, boys. Charge!"

Slocum heard the command from his right side. A quick

glance confirmed what this really meant. He whirled left and got off all four shots from the rifle before coming up empty. As the hammer fell on the empty chamber, a wry smile crossed his face. Four shots and he had brought down two of the outlaws.

He turned back to the other direction as those rustlers advanced. And from the corner of his eye he saw three others advancing from the depths of the canyon.

All he had left were a couple rounds in his six-gun. He vowed to make them count.

5

The range was extreme for a six-gun, but Slocum did what he could by giving a bit of arc to every shot. He thought he scared one of the rustlers, then his hammer fell on a spent round. He was out of ammunition. Reaching down, he drew the thick-bladed knife he sheathed in the top of his boot. It wouldn't do any good, but he felt better having some weapon as the outlaws advanced on him.

He took cover as a fusillade ripped through the air, then realized the shots came from the direction Blassingame had taken. He couldn't believe the foreman had gotten enough strength to come back to his rescue. A quick glance over his shoulder showed a lone rider galloping forth, wildly firing a rifle.

It wasn't Blassingame. It was Tom Garvin.

"Damned fool," Slocum muttered. He rose and tried to wave off the cowboy, but Garvin paid him no heed.

Sure that he would see Garvin blown out of the saddle, Slocum watched in rapt fascination as the young man kept firing and kept hitting his target. Slocum had seen more than one Wild West Show and seldom had any of those trick shooters been more accurate. It was as if every round Garvin fired winged or brought down an outlaw. When he rushed past where Slocum crouched behind a rock, Slocum saw how Garvin held his black rope in his teeth and somehow fired and loaded his rifle at a dead gallop.

In a few minutes an eerie silence fell over the canyon. Garvin rode back, the rope still between his teeth.

"On the rim, watch for snipers!"

Garvin heard Slocum's warning and looked up. Almost casually, he raised his rifle and fired. Slocum gaped as the rifleman high atop the wall stood straight, then fell stiff as a board all the way to the canyon floor. He didn't doubt the outlaw had been killed instantly by Garvin's impossible shot. The fall was only icing on the cake.

"You still in one piece, Slocum?" Garvin took the rope from his mouth and held it in his left hand while still clutching the rifle in his right.

"I am, thanks to you," Slocum said. He looked around for sign that the cowboy hadn't finished off the rustlers but saw no movement anywhere on the canyon floor.

Aware of how naked he felt without ammunition, Slocum walked to the nearest outlaw and plucked his rifle from his nerveless hands. A second one had been drilled smack dab between the eyes. Slocum took his rifle, too.

"Ain't much use strippin' all of 'em, is there?"

Slocum walked back to where Garvin beamed at him. He restlessly ran his hand over the black rope with the silver thread running the length, then dropped it, formed a loop, and began spinning as expertly as any cowboy Slocum had ever seen.

"What happened to Blassingame?"

"He fell off his horse at the mouth of the canyon. I seen him and came in to find what the fuss was. Reckoned you needed some help."

"I needed more than that. I needed a whole damn company of cavalry," Slocum said. He smiled ruefully. "Looks like

I got the next best thing. That was about the dumbest thing you've done since trying to ride that piebald mustang."

Tom Garvin scowled, as if trying to decide if Slocum was making fun of him. Then an arrogance settled on him like a well-fitting coat.

"I was what the doctor ordered. Pulled your bacon out of the fire."

"We have to get Blassingame tended to," Slocum said.

"Why don't you find where these owlhoots left their horses and get a couple?"

"Good idea," Slocum said. He went to his felled horse and pulled his gear out from under the dead weight. Slinging the saddle over his shoulder, he started walking deeper into the canyon.

"You get all saddled up and we kin take this itty-bitty herd back to the Bar M," Garvin said.

Slocum saw nothing wrong with that. They had to go in that direction to get Blassingame, so why not drive the two-dozen beeves along with them?

He found where the outlaws had left their horses, chose the best, riffled through the saddlebags, and took a few dollars. But there wasn't much else worth claiming. He saddled and rode to the far end of the canyon. As he had thought, a tall, narrow wall of rock hid an exit from what otherwise looked to be a box canyon.

"Come on, Slocum, 'less you want me to do all yer work for you!"

Garvin laughed joyfully, swung his black rope, and whacked a few bovine butts and got the herd moving.

Slocum positioned himself to the rear on the far side of the herd, and they made quick work of moving the cattle back from the canyon and onto the range.

"I'll take care of Blassingame," Slocum said when they got to the fallen foreman. "You go on and get the beeves to the corral."

"Think I kin git my job back?"

"I'll speak for you," Slocum said. He heaved Blassingame to a sitting position. The foreman had taken quite a tumble from his horse but was still conscious. The foreman's eyelids flickered.

"Him? That Garvin? That the son of a bitch what saved us?"

"Sure enough," Slocum said, heaving the foreman to his feet. Once more he got the man astride his horse. This time Blassingame rode with his eyes fixed on Garvin's back all the way to the ranch house.

Magnuson stood on the porch, hands on his hips, watching Garvin and Slocum get the cattle into the fenced field behind the barn. Blassingame rode over. The rancher caught him as he slid from the saddle. Putting an arm around his foreman's shoulders, Magnuson guided the wounded man to the steps.

By the time Slocum rode over, the rancher had the story from Blassingame.

"That wet-behind-the-ears boy, he saved you both?" Magnuson fixed Slocum with a steely gaze.

"Can't praise him highly enough," Slocum said. "I was a goner. A dozen rustlers had me dead to rights, and they'd already shot up Blassingame."

"That's not your horse."

"The rustlers shot mine. This is one of theirs. Got another, too. Garvin killed two of them, maybe more."

Tom Garvin rode over. He ran his hand back and forth over the black rope fastened in a loop to his saddle. Slocum was glad the cowboy understood that it wasn't his place to say anything. Garvin sat and waited.

"You want your job back?" Magnuson looked from Blassingame to Slocum and then at Garvin. "Jed agrees you deserve another chance. Slocum's in agreement."

"Not sure I want the job," Garvin said, "after the way I was treated." Seeing Magnuson bristle, Garvin hurried on. "But it's a decent offer, and I'll take you up on it, sir."

"You watch your step. Saving those steers saved your job."

Garvin and Magnuson traded a few more remarks, but Slocum paid them no attention. He saw Christine standing in the doorway, leaning against the jamb, hip cocked provocatively, hand resting on it. The tiny smile she gave was just for him. Slocum found himself wanting to dismount and go tell her pa what he and his daughter had been up to. Magnuson would likely try to fire him, but it might be worth it.

Then Christine stepped out and called, "Papa, the bed is ready for Mr. Blassingame. We can get him fixed up in nothing flat."

Magnuson started to say something more to Garvin, then spun and helped his foreman up the steps. Slocum envied Blassingame, the way the woman put her arm around his waist and helped him along. She gave Slocum one quick glance over her shoulder, then guided the foreman into the house and disappeared. Magnuson slammed the door with a finality that caused Slocum to jump.

"This is my lucky day," Garvin said, laughing. "I get fired, then I save a whole passel of cows and chase off rustlers before gettin' my job back."

Slocum looked hard at the boy.

"How'd you come to be riding by when you did?"

Garvin shrugged.

"That was a damned fool thing to do, too, charging smack into the outlaws the way you did. How'd you come to chase off the entire gang? They had to know you weren't leading a posse."

"I told you, Slocum. Luck. You ain't gainsayin' it, now are you? Saved your hide." Garvin looked at the closed ranch house door. "And his life, too. Not sure that was such a good thing."

"Blassingame's not so bad," Slocum said. "Worked for worse. He's got a hair-trigger temper's all."

"How much more does a foreman make than a range rider like us?"

The question took Slocum by surprise. Garvin was showing ambition that had never surfaced before. He had done nothing but work hard to learn his job as a cowboy and never had mentioned any interest in doing anything more.

"You might as well wish for Hashknife's job," Slocum said. "Blassingame and Magnuson have been a team for nigh on ten years. Leastways, that's what I've heard."

During pillow talk with Christine, he had learned a great deal about Magnuson and Jed Blassingame. She had wanted to impress him with what good men they were. She obviously thought as highly of the foreman as she did her pa, maybe because he was around and taking care of her almost as much when Magnuson was traveling on business.

"A blind leper could cook as good as Hashknife," Garvin said. "Bein' foreman's a job I could come to like, bossin' folks around and not havin' to do much."

"He got shot up because we went after the strays," Slocum said.

"Blassingame got paid more for his day's work than you did, Slocum." Garvin shook his head, tugged on the reins, and got his new horse headed for the barn.

Slocum trailed him, wondering at the change he saw in Garvin's attitude. There was hardly any gratitude for getting his job back. Even after saving the foreman's life, Tom Garvin might not have been rehired. Magnuson was a stiff son of a bitch with a broomstick crammed up his ass. It was a tribute as much to Slocum as it was to Blassingame that he had offered Garvin his job back.

"Yes, sir, Slocum, things is lookin' up for this stud cowboy," Garvin said, kicking open the bunkhouse door. He heaved his gear around onto his old bunk. For a moment he stared at the saddlebags resting on the bunk.

Slocum wondered if he was going to ask for another bed. Garvin had complained before about this one being bedbug ridden. That was hardly the only infested one, but he hadn't seen fit to burn his mattress and make a new one.

Garvin turned and faced Slocum.

"You got any gun-cleanin' supplies?"

"Why'd you want any? For your rifle? You left that with your saddle. You'd better get your horse curried and fed before you think on cleaning it."

"I mean my six-shooter," the cowboy said. He opened the saddlebags and pulled out a blued-steel Smith & Wesson.

"You take that off one of the outlaws?"

"Why not? He wasn't gonna need it no more." Garvin spun it around on his trigger finger and stopped its swing pointed straight at Slocum. "Bang, yer dead."

Slocum batted the barrel aside.

"Don't ever point that gun at anybody you don't intend to shoot."

"Aw, I was just funnin' with you, Slocum. How'd you get so sour all of a sudden?"

"I always get that way when people who don't know how to handle a six-shooter point it at me."

"I kin learn. Hell, I'm learnin' ever'thing about ranchin'. Like I said, Blassingame's job'll be mine real soon. Can't be all that hard tellin' the hands to go rope and brand and round up cows. They're danged stupid."

Slocum wasn't sure if he meant the cows or the cowboys. As cocky as Garvin had become, it could have been either— or both. For all his fiery temper, Jed Blassingame never ragged on his men as being stupid, even when they did stupid things. He wasn't above egging them on, as he had done with Garvin to ride the piebald, but he didn't make a point of their mistakes.

"You know how to clean a six-gun?" Slocum went to his bunk and pulled out a box under it holding gear he didn't want to carry out on the range. He took the wire brush and solvent, held them for a moment, then passed them to Garvin. "You need a rag. Clean out the gunpowder in the barrel, then be sure everything's oiled, but not too much.

You don't want to drown the mechanism or you'll end up with dust clogging the trigger."

"Take my horse to the barn, will you, while I clean my new piece." Garvin spun it again, then made like he was shooting outlaws again.

Slocum left the cowboy to his chore, gathered the reins on the horses, and led them to the barn. He unsaddled his new horse and examined the hooves, shoes, and teeth. While sorry he'd had his last mount shot down, this wasn't a bad replacement. The brand on the hindquarters was indistinct, as if the previous owner had tried running the brand. Which he probably had. Why stop with stealing cattle?

He had barely curried the horse and poured some grain into a nosebag when the gunshot rang out. Slocum ran to the barn door, hand on his own six-shooter, aware that he had neglected to reload. That had been on his mind until Garvin distracted him, wanting to use the cleaning supplies for his captured six-gun.

"Who's shooting up the place?" Magnuson stood on the porch, shotgun in his hand. He pushed Christine back into the house, then stomped into the yard to look around. "You fire your gun, Slocum?"

"Nope," he said, heading for the bunkhouse. "The shot came from inside."

"Inside? Nobody's there. All the hands are out on the range right now."

"Except Garvin. He was cleaning his pistol."

"What consarned fool gave that greenhorn a gun? Tarnation." Magnuson stormed to the bunkhouse, pushed open the door with the shotgun barrel, and peered inside cautiously. "Son of a bitch. He's upped and killed himself."

Slocum crowded past the rancher. He sucked in his breath. Tom Garvin lay on the floor, his shirt stained with blood from the bullet wound to his heart.

6

Slocum dropped to his knees beside the supine man and pressed fingers into his throat. He looked up at Magnuson and said, "He's still alive."

"Hell's bells, there's no way I can take care of a wound like that." Magnuson poked with the muzzle of the shotgun to move part of Garvin's bullet-holed shirt away from the wound. "During the war I worked as a medic's assistant and learned to do damn near anything he could, but this isn't something I can deal with."

"You took care of Blassingame," Slocum said.

"His wounds were nothing compared to this." Magnuson shook his head. "Hate like hell to let him die here, but there's not much else to do."

Slocum slid the black rope Garvin fancied so under the man's body and hoisted him erect using it. Garvin moaned, and his eyelids fluttered but otherwise showed no sign of life.

"Where are you going with him?"

"To the wagon. I can get him to the doctor in town."

"Abbey? That old derelict?" Magnuson sucked on his teeth a moment, then nodded. "If Garvin lives long enough,

Abbey's good enough a sawbones to save him. I've seen him work miracles." He heaved a deep, shuddering sigh. "I've seen him so drunk he could barely hit the floor with his own puke, too."

Slocum bent forward and settled Garvin on his back. The man's feeble stirring convinced him it was worth the trip to town, even if it wasn't likely to be as pleasurable as the last he had taken with Christine. The return trip was likely to be even less agreeable since he didn't see how Garvin could survive the short miles to town, much less a doctor who tippled.

"I'll get the team," Magnuson said. He rushed past Slocum and his burden.

By the time Slocum staggered up and swung his load into the wagon, Magnuson had finished hitching up the horses.

"Stay on the far left side of the road as you go into town. The potholes are smaller, and the sides are built up different. Makes for a smoother ride."

"Thanks," Slocum said. "I'll be back as quick as I can."

"Have him buried in the town cemetery," Magnuson said as Slocum snapped the reins and got the wagon rolling. "No reason to fetch the corpse back."

As Slocum passed the ranch house, he saw Christine peering from a window. She looked drawn, apprehensive. He touched the brim of his hat to her—this was all he dared do with her pa watching every bump and lurch of the wagon as it left the yard and got on the road to town. Slocum didn't know if he eased Christine's worry. Her pa would report back what had happened. It was odd for Slocum to find anyone who cared for him, who showed concern for his well-being.

He'd be a damned fool not to marry her. All the way into Central City he thought of her, her soft caresses on his face and the lusty moves of her hips, the soft breath against his chest afterward. Remembering all this kept him from wondering if Tom Garvin was going to die before he reached town, not that Dr. Abbey was likely to perform any kind of miracle with a wound that severe. The only thing Slocum knew for a fact was how lucky Garvin was not to have killed himself outright.

Nobody paid him any attention as he rolled down the middle of the narrow main street. The sun was sinking low, making driving hard, even with his hat pulled down. He had to twist his head around a mite to keep the failing light from shining through the bullet hole in his hat brim. He drew back on the reins and brought the team to a halt outside the doctor's office. A shingle swung fitfully in the evening breeze. LLOYD ABBEY, MD, it read in flaking gold letters on a white-washed board.

Slocum wrapped the reins around the brake and vaulted to the ground. His legs almost gave out. All during the ride into town, he had been tensed up, his feet pressing hard against the front of the wagon box. Now that he had to support himself, those muscles refused to move right, all knotted up. Hobbling, he went directly into the doctor's office.

A small, peevish-looking man with thinning white hair looked up from a book open on the desk in front of him.

"Don't you know how to knock? Get out of here, close the door, and leave me be." Abbey turned up the kerosene lamp to shine more light on his book as he turned back to it.

"Man's wounded bad," Slocum said.

The doctor heaved a sigh of disgust, carefully inserted a bookmark to save his place, and closed the book. He pushed back and pointed to a table in the middle of the room.

"Set yourself down and let me look at those legs. You been crippled up like this long?"

"Not me—Tom Garvin. Out in the wagon."

Abbey made vague shooing motions as if chasing away flies.

"Can he walk?"

"Caught a bullet through the heart."

This produced a look of utter disgust. Abbey turned back to his desk.

"My cousin's no-good son runs the undertaking parlor. On the edge of town, out near the cemetery. Convenient for him, I'd say, and it might be the only smart thing he ever did, picking that location for his store. That's what he calls it. An undertaker's store." He snorted and started to sit once more.

Slocum left, grabbed the ends of the rope around Garvin, and heaved him onto his back again. It took some maneuvering to get through the door and put the wounded cowboy onto the examination table.

"I told you I don't deal with dead bodies. Not intentionally. That's—"

"He's still alive." Slocum took Garvin's wrist and lifted. The cowboy tried to feebly yank away as he moaned.

"Then tell me that. Don't spin a tall tale about him getting shot through the heart." Dr. Abbey settled pince-nez glasses on the end of his Roman nose and bent over Garvin. Delicate fingers pried loose the shirt glued to a heaving chest by dried blood.

"Can you do anything for him?"

"You were right. Shot through the heart. Bullet still in him?" Abbey looked up over the top of his eyeglasses.

"Far as I know."

Dr. Abbey reached over and took a long, slender metal tool like an icepick and began probing with it. After a tiny click sounded, he looked up.

"Found the slug. What I haven't found is his heart."

"What do you mean? He doesn't have one?"

"It's not where it should be, that's for certain. Get out of here and fetch a drink."

"For you?" Slocum remembered what Magnuson had said. He got a snort for an answer.

"You must work for that old reprobate Mordecai Magnuson. He's the only one who thinks I'm a drunkard. Get yourself out of my office while I work. I meant that *you* looked like you could use a drink."

Slocum saw the doctor turn back to Garvin and begin peeling back his shirt preparatory to pouring carbolic acid all over the wound. He backed to the door, then left. The sight of blood didn't bother him. He had seen more spilled during the war than he cared to remember, and some of it had been brutal. During one shelling in the Battle of the Wilderness, a Yankee cannonball had taken off the head of the soldier standing next to him. One instant he had been yelling insults at the enemy and the next he was geysering blood an improbable height into the air from his headless body.

Slocum had seen blood aplenty but the way Garvin had shot himself wore on him. He should have made sure the man realized the six-shooter had to be unloaded. And how was it his heart wasn't in the right place? Slocum had never heard of such a thing.

The night air wrapped itself around him, chilling him. Only then did he realize how he had been sweating like a pig. Shaking all over, he got himself back to feeling halfway normal. His legs were still knotted up, but walking down the street to the saloon loosened him up. Light spilled from the open doors and invited him in.

There wasn't much more than the sound of a piano player banging at the keys and trying to sing. It took Slocum a couple seconds to even identify the song. When he did, it took him back to the war. "Tentin' on the Old Campground" raised memories he didn't care to relive. He considered finding another saloon where the piano player wasn't inclined to play old war songs, then decided he could endure the last few notes. He went to the bar and leaned forward, elbows resting on a well-polished wood surface. The entire section of bar was a Brunswick and mighty fancy for a cow town.

"What's your poison?" The barkeep cinched up the cord around his waist so his apron wouldn't flop about.

"The piano player's going to get lead poisoning if he doesn't play something else."

"Can't rightly say what else he does know. Been playin'

that same ole song over and over. That and the 'Yellow Rose of Texas.'" Seeing Slocum's expression, he pursed his lips, then nodded. "All right, wait a second, mister." The barkeep roared for the piano player to pick something livelier.

"'Camptown Races' suit you?"

"It does," Slocum said. "So would a shot of whiskey."

"Trade whiskey or some of Billy Taylor's Finest? I kin fix you up with one of my special mixed drinks. I'm the best damn drink mixer in town and do a tasty Peach French Fizz."

"Billy Taylor's been a friend of mine for quite a while."

"He doesn't disappoint any of my customers," the barkeep said, pouring a shot from a squat brown bottle with the proper label.

Slocum sipped, nodded approval, then downed the drink in a single grateful gulp. It might have been actual whiskey all the way from San Francisco. Didn't matter much, though, since it left a warmth in his belly that slowly spread to steal away his aches and pains. With the piano blaring out its off-key song that didn't remind him of the war, Slocum was on his way to feeling halfway human.

The mellowness went away when he heard a voice behind him.

"Didn't expect to see you again, Slocum."

He looked up but couldn't catch sight of the man in the back bar mirror. It was always like Wiley Pendergast to be cautious. That was how he had stayed alive so long. That was how he had avoided catching one of Slocum's bullets.

"Thought you'd be in prison somewhere. Yuma, maybe."

"Yeah, you'd think that, the way you turned me over to that federal marshal."

"My memory's a tad different on that score," Slocum said, remembering that he carried an empty six-shooter at his side. "You tried to get him to arrest me. I can't be held responsible if he got confused and nabbed you instead."

"Not as if I hadn't done enough for a federal lawman to get on my trail." Pendergast sidled up to the bar next to Slocum.

He hadn't changed in the three years since they'd rustled cattle together down in Arizona Territory. If anything, he was uglier, but his face still carried a touch of baby fat, making him look like he was in his teens. Slocum knew he was over thirty. He just didn't show it then or now. All the miles on the trail, all the hours under the burning sun, none of it had furrowed Pendergast's face with lines or even the weathering most honest cowboys showed after a season on the range.

"You get caught?" Slocum wanted the outlaw to keep talking. If it came down to gunplay, he was a goner.

"Left a federal marshal floatin' facedown in the Colorado River. Lit out for California, worked my way up the coast to Oregon. Thought I found you there workin' on an Appaloosa ranch. Turned out to be somebody who just looked like you."

"Too bad."

"It was too bad for him. I killed him by mistake." Pendergast shook his head sadly. "That was a waste of a good bullet. But it did change me."

"How's that?"

"I gave up huntin' you, Slocum. Turned my attention to other pursuits, you might say."

"Those Appaloosas were too inviting to pass up?" Slocum knew the answer by Pendergast's chuckle. The man had gone into horse thieving.

"Thinkin' back on it, that bullet wasn't wasted at all. I got fifteen mighty fine horses and sold them for a thousand dollars."

"Gambling? Booze? Whores?"

"You know me too well, Slocum. All three, though the whores took most of my money. Made me bound and determined to start afresh. And I did. I worked my way eastward, found a bank or two that wasn't too careful with how they stashed their money—one banker actually took the greenbacks home with him every night and tucked them into his mattress because he mistrusted his own safe. Can you believe that?"

"The Bar M cattle are quite a draw for you," Slocum said.

"You didn't recognize me out there in the canyon, did you? You was too surprised when I come up behind you a minute ago."

"Shouldn't be any more surprised when I step on a rattler. You lost a couple men out there."

Wiley Pendergast made a shooing motion with his left hand. Slocum saw how he kept his right near the Colt holstered on his hip.

"Those boys are a dime a dozen. Now, them cows you stole from me, that's another matter."

"They were Bar M beeves, not yours."

"I talked this over with a lawyer once, and he told me strays out on the range are for the takin'. Anybody what finds them can keep 'em. Sounded all legal to me."

"No more legal than to run the brands."

"Bar M is an easy one. I can make a Bar Star Bar out of it mighty quick. Over the years, I've learned some metal working and am a fair smithy when the situation calls for it."

"Set up shop and shoe horses. You'll live longer."

"Now there you go, Slocum, threatenin' me again, jist like you did down in Yuma. To show you I don't hold a grudge, I'm gonna do you a favor." Pendergast stepped back a pace and turned so he could throw down. "I'm invitin' you to take the place of one of them gents you killed."

Slocum blinked in surprise. It took him a couple seconds to get his wits about him since this was the last thing he had expected from Wiley Pendergast.

"I've got a job," Slocum said carefully.

Pendergast grinned, showing a broken front tooth. He rested his hand on the butt of his Colt and tapped nervously with his trigger finger. Slocum considered how he could rush him before he cleared leather and didn't see any way open unless he heaved the shot glass at him. Pendergast wasn't the kind who distracted that easily.

"Why, so you do, so you do. Just happens this fits in real

nice with my plans of taking a hundred head of cattle off that range."

"All legal like, the way the lawyer told you?" Slocum couldn't help smiling at the notion. Pay a lawyer enough and they'd say whatever you wanted. The way the law was administered in most places, the lawyer who did the most jury bribing won.

"You always were quick on the uptake, Slocum. The way I see it, you owe me. Not for my dead partners. Hell, I can't even remember their names now. No, you owe me for sic-cing the marshal on me in Yuma. You owe me for too many years of trackin' you down."

"The horses you stole up in Oregon should have been pay enough."

"A reasonable man might think that," Pendergast said, his voice getting an edge to it, "but I ain't never been a rea-sonable man. You're gonna help me get those beeves."

"Or?"

"Now, Slocum, you know me better than that. I don't make threats. I keep my promises, and I promise you'll regret it if you don't snap to when I tell you." Pendergast stepped forward and pushed Slocum into the bar. This would have been enough to have Slocum reaching for his Colt Navy in another circumstance.

But not with six empty chambers in his pistol.

Pendergast stopped at the door and smiled. There wasn't any humor in it, then he disappeared into the night.

"You want another?" the barkeep asked. His voice trem-bled just a mite.

"I've got to see about a dead man," Slocum said. He stepped into the cool evening and looked around for Pendergast or any of his gang. The street was as quiet as a cemetery.

He headed for Dr. Abbey's office to get the rest of the bad news before heading back to the Bar M.

7

Slocum took a deep breath as he went into the doctor's office. Dr. Abbey was covered in blood as he stood over the table where Garvin stretched out, unmoving.

"I got it out," the doctor said, reaching to a tin plate. He lifted the bullet and held it between bloodstained thumb and forefinger before tossing it back into the pan with a sharp rattle. "One of the easiest extractions I ever made. Drove in the probe, scouted the periphery, and got forceps on the slug. Came right out."

"I'll take him now," Slocum said.

"You willing to pay for his funeral?" Abbey asked sharply.

"He doesn't have any family, so I reckon so." Slocum walked over, then stopped dead in his tracks. He looked at the doctor.

"You move him, and he dies. He's still alive, and if I can venture an opinion, he's rallying."

"Getting stronger?"

"Exactly that," Dr. Abbey said.

"But the bullet went into his heart." Slocum saw how the

doctor had a bandage over the wound. "Nobody lives through that."

"True, nobody can, but there's one thing wrong with what you just said. The bullet didn't go through his heart. His heart is on the right side. I've heard tell of such a thing but never saw it 'fore today. Oh, the wound was serious, no question about that. But it didn't drill through his heart, though it would have in you or me." Abbey squinted at Slocum. "Unless you want to tell me your heart's on the wrong side, too."

"Don't think so," Slocum said. "He's going to live?"

"Unless you insist on moving him. Give him a week or so to recover before loading him back into that wagon. You can tell Mordecai that he's not going to get a decent day's work out of this one for a month."

Slocum didn't know what to say.

"And you tell Mordecai that he can pay me direct, since this is one of his boys." Abbey grinned wolfishly. "Be even better if he sends that daughter of his to pay the bill. She's the only one on that ranch that bothers to bathe—and is the only one it wouldn't matter to me."

"I'll tell Mr. Magnuson," Slocum said. "And I'll bring back clothes for him." He couldn't believe Garvin had survived such a nasty wound. Men ran several paces, sometimes more, in the heat of battle filled full of holes, but they eventually keeled over dead. Garvin was something special.

Slocum reached to pull the black rope from under the man, only to have a surprisingly strong hand grip his wrist. Garvin's eyes flickered open and fixed on him. Words formed on his lips, but Garvin was too weak to speak. He didn't have to. Slocum got the message.

"Don't touch the rope." Dr. Abbey gently moved Slocum's hand away.

Slocum dropped the rope onto the table beside Garvin and stepped back.

"Now that's the second most astounding thing I ever did see," the doctor said. He took Garvin's hand and checked the pulse. "The first being him living through my surgery, of course. But to be this strong so soon after . . ." He put the wrist on the table so it wouldn't fall off and stretch the sewn-up wound in Garvin's chest. "If all my patients recovered this fast, might be some of them would see fit to pay me."

Slocum went to the wagon and climbed into the driver's box. He didn't know whether to return to the Bar M or head in the opposite direction and keep driving until he had put a hundred miles behind him. It wasn't natural for Tom Garvin to heal up as fast as he had. It wasn't natural to be so damned lucky, if shooting yourself cleaning a six-shooter could ever be called good luck. But he hadn't died.

Slocum snapped the reins and got the team moving. He wasn't thinking clearly, but when he realized he was on the road back to the ranch, he knew the reason. That was where Christine was.

Letting his thoughts drift, Slocum took the turns in the road and didn't try to avoid the worst of the potholes. In the dark, it was almost impossible anyway. The moon would rise in another hour, but it wouldn't give enough light, not with the thin wisps of clouds forming into heavier ones that promised rain. Slocum reflected on how the rains that the land had been denied for long weeks always came when a trail drive started. Make the cowboys and cattle as miserable as possible. That seemed like some inscrutable law of Nature.

As he drove along, his reverie died away as small sounds demanded his attention. He glimpsed movement out of the corner of his eye more than once. Even a swift turn and steady gaze did not reveal anything in the dark. At first he thought an ambitious wolf might be stalking him—or his team. When the feeling of being watched did not go away, he knew it wasn't a wolf paralleling the road. A wolf would have given up after a mile or two.

A human wouldn't.

Slocum's anger rose as he thought about Pendergast and

their meeting in the saloon. The last thing he wanted was to jeopardize his position at the Bar M. Unlike Tom Garvin, he had no designs on taking the foreman's job. He wanted something more precious.

Christine. The name rolled over and over in his head like the most beautiful song he had ever heard. If the saloon piano player had only plinked a single key and sang that name the rest of the night, he couldn't have pleased Slocum more.

Slocum swung around fast, looking at the road behind. He thought he saw shadows moving in trees off to one side but couldn't be sure. He touched the butt of his Colt, remembering he was out of ammo. If he'd carried a full cylinder in his trusty six-shooter, he would have returned to find if he was being followed. Instead, he snapped the reins and got the team pulling a bit harder. The horses weren't happy; neither was he.

His mood changed as he pulled in to park the rig behind the barn. A single light burned in the ranch house. Christine was up late. After putting the horses in their stalls, he made sure the wagon was secure, worn wood blocks under the front wheels since it was parked on a slight incline. Slocum hurried to Christine's window and peered in, ready to tap on the pane. Luck rode with him. He had almost rapped on the window when he saw Jed Blassingame in Christine's bed. The foreman tossed and turned and finally flopped flat on his back.

His groans of pain came through the closed window. Slocum watched as Christine came in, robe pulled around her slender form. She poured Blassingame some water and added a drop or two of medicine. Slocum thought it must be laudanum. The foreman's injuries must have been more severe than anyone thought at first.

Even if they weren't, his recovery wasn't as amazing as Tom Garvin's.

Christine made sure Blassingame had finished the water and put the glass on the bedside table, then turned down the lamp. As she did, she looked out and saw Slocum. She jumped as if he had poked her with a stick. A quick glance back assured her that Blassingame had not seen the nocturnal visitor, then she hurried from the room.

Slocum moved as silently as a shadow crossing another shadow and waited at the rear porch. Christine came out as silently as he had.

"John, you frightened me!"

"Didn't mean to. Just got back from town."

"How is Tom?"

He took her arm and steered her from the ranch house.

"Come on out to the barn. I don't want your pa waving around that shotgun of his if he overhears us."

"Oh, and what might he overhear?" She took a deep breath and pulled back her shoulders. Her robe opened, revealing a cotton nightgown that should have been chaste. Slocum saw how her nipples had hardened and pressed into the thin fabric.

"Me telling you how much I love you," he said. He kissed her. She tensed, then melted into the circle of his arms. Her body pressed warmly against his and then began a more insistent movement as she wrapped one leg around his and began rubbing her crotch against his thigh.

"Think there's a pile of straw out in the barn?" she asked, her breath hot in his ear.

"We can make do if there isn't," he said.

Arm around her waist, he steered her toward the dark barn. They went through a small side door and looked around. She pulled free and dashed toward the ladder leading to the loft. He followed and got a tantalizing sight as her bare legs flashed in the darkness, scissoring as she went up.

He trailed her, enjoying the sight, even if it was mostly hidden in the shadows of her robe and nightgown. By the time he reached the loft, Christine had shucked off the robe and laid it on a pile of hay intended for the horses. She threw out her arms and fell back onto the robe, slowly drew up her knees, and scooted her nightgown out of the way.

Her spread knees looked like gun sights and the target was the dark triangle so wantonly offered to him.

"Open the loft doors," she said. "The moon's rising, and I want you to make love to me in the moonlight."

Slocum flung the doors open and turned back to see an entirely naked woman stretched out invitingly for him. She held out her arms, and he dropped to his knees. She reached over and began stripping off his clothes as moonlight played between the shadows and cast silver pools on her perfect white skin.

He caught one nipple and rolled the hard bud between his forefinger and thumb. She moaned softly. He repeated the effort on the other side, then bent low and suckled. He drew the rubbery tip between his lips and tended it with lips and teeth and tongue until Christine writhed about under him.

He kissed the deep valley between her breasts and moved lower to her navel, where he dallied for only a moment before plunging even lower into forbidden territory now open to him. Tongue laving along the sex flaps, Slocum was treated to suddenly going deaf and blind. The woman's thighs clamped down hard on either side of his head, holding him in place. There was nowhere else he wanted to go.

Tongue thrusting in and out, licking up and down, he caused her to arch her back and moan so loud that the horses in the stalls below began to turn fitful. He didn't let up his oral assault on her pink gates. His tongue slid deeper into her and rolled about. Her fingers laced through his lank, dark hair to hold him in place.

Then she tugged hard and pulled him away.

"What's wrong?" he asked.

"That's sooo good," she said in a sex husky voice, "but I want more of you in me. Lots more!" She tugged and pulled him up along her body as her knees rose on either side of his chest.

When the throbbing end of his organ bumped into the

area where his mouth had been seconds earlier, the woman let out a tiny shriek, then bit her lip to keep from even louder outcries.

"You like that?" He positioned himself and moved his hips forward a few inches. The purpled end of his manhood parted the nether lips and sank a ways into her. "You like this better?" He teased her with small movements, an inch in fast and then a slow retreat the same distance until he saw a flush rising on her chest.

The moonlight turned her into an angel, a fairy fluttering down to deliver only pure lusty delight.

He levered his hips forward and slowly inserted himself balls deep into her willing core. The heat and wetness around him proved more stimulating than he expected. She was turned on and communicated this to him by tensing and relaxing strong inner muscles. He was wetly, warmly squeezed and then released.

Pressure built in his balls, but Slocum remained hidden full length in her center, not moving more than he had to. This drove Christine's passions even higher.

"Oh, John, you're making me crazy for you. I feel you inside. So big, so hard, soooo—"

She gasped and arched her back, cramming her hips down hard as if to split herself in two on his fleshy knife. This was more than Slocum could handle. The grip around him was increasing in power and desire. He began thrusting. He tried to keep a steady rhythm and succeeded for a minute or two, then found himself unable to do anything but stroke wildly. All his desires exploded as he spilled his seed in her.

Christine tried to hold back a long, loud cry of release and failed. Cattle in nearby feed pens lowed in response, a dog barked, and the horses below in the barn began kicking at their stalls. Her fingernails cut into his broad back, and they crammed themselves together at the crotch as hard as they could. And then, passions expended, they sank down to lie side by side in the moonlight.

Sweat beaded Christine's forehead like liquid silver beads. Slocum reached out and gently whisked them away. She smiled, just a little, eyes still closed. Then she pursed her lips. He kissed them. And just before sunup they finished again.

"Oh, John, I have to get back to the house. Papa will be up anytime now, and I could never explain."

"If he gives you any woe, I'll talk to him."

Christine sat up, eyes wide. She started to say something, then shook her head. Words finally formed.

"He'd kill you." After a moment's consideration, she added, "Or you'd have to kill him. I wouldn't want that."

He started to say that he would make an honest woman of her, no matter what her pa thought, but she pulled the robe from under them, sending him rolling. When he sat up, she had the robe pulled tightly around her and was heading down the ladder. With only her head still poking up into the loft, she blew him a kiss and then vanished.

Slocum lay back, then found himself warmed by the first rays of dawn. He rummaged about in the hay and found his clothes, finally pulling on his boots and dropping down the ladder just as Mordecai Magnuson came in.

"You're up early, Slocum. Tendin' the horses?" Magnuson looked around and saw no work had been done yet.

"Just rolled in from town." Slocum told him of Garvin's brush with death.

"That son of a bitch has the worst luck ever followed by good. No, better than good. Never heard of nobody shot in the heart—shooting himself in the heart!—and living to tell of it." Magnuson grabbed a shovel and tossed it to Slocum. "Get on with the work. Finish it all and get yourself cleaned up if you want to go."

"Go where?" Slocum asked, bending to the task of mucking the nearest stall.

"There's a square dance tonight over at the Norton spread."

"What's the occasion?" Slocum went cold inside when he saw the broad smile on Magnuson's face.

"I reckon Josh Junior's got somethin' he wants to ask my daughter. And if he doesn't, then it's a big dance to celebrate all of us getting our herds to market. Drive starts day after the dance. That's why I think he wants to ask her now, before we're all on the trail."

Magnuson left whistling off-key. Slocum stood with a shovel of shit in his hand and a taste of ashes in his mouth.

8

"Dammit, don't like being shorthanded this close to the drive," Magnuson groused. He turned in the saddle and glared at Slocum. "You're not pullin' your weight today, Slocum. Something eating you?"

Slocum almost told the rancher about him and Christine, then bit back the words. They had worked under the hot sun all morning. He had thought hard work would burn out the fury growing in him that Magnuson considered his daughter a fair match with the younger Norton boy. Christine didn't have a good word to say for him, and their marriage would be loveless, an arranged union to combine two large ranches rather than consider the feelings of the couple.

Slocum snorted. He didn't doubt Josh Junior was all in favor of the marriage. Christine was a lovely woman, feisty and determined. Slocum had the feeling he was a better match for the rancher's daughter than anyone from the Norton spread. Although he didn't know the boy, Junior, from accounts, had grown up feeling like royalty. Too much money, not enough challenge in his life. At least that was how Christine portrayed him, and Slocum believed her.

"Anxious to get on the trail," Slocum lied to the rancher.

"We got a good herd this year. Grass was plentiful early in the season, and you and that Garvin fellow kept the rustlers from stealin' me blind."

"Too bad he can't go on the drive," Slocum said.

"Doesn't look too promisin' for Jed either," Magnuson said, turning somber. "He's hurtin' somethin' fierce. Christine's a good nurse, but she's done all she can for him. It didn't look like it at the time, but those damned rustlers about did him in. I'm thinkin' Dr. Abbey might fix him up like he did Garvin."

Slocum didn't bother saying anything about the miracle of a man having his heart on the wrong side and how this had saved his life. Tom Garvin was a curious mix of good and bad luck, as Magnuson had said that morning. When a man's luck ran good, everyone crowded close, but Slocum was coming to look at Garvin as a jinx. He wasn't an especially superstitious man, but there was no harm in keeping his distance from Garvin should his bad luck explode out and rain down on anyone too close.

"We'll do all right," Slocum said. He wanted to tell Magnuson about his feelings for Christine, but the rancher suddenly wheeled his horse and galloped away, leaving behind a cloud of choking dust. Slocum spat, then turned back to his work.

By late afternoon, they had brought in the sicklier of the cows to examine. If they couldn't make the drive, they'd be slaughtered and sold in town right away. Slocum cut out those heifers that would build the herd for the following year and gave orders to keep them apart. Steers and older cattle only were part of the herd going to the railhead.

"Hey, Jonesy, come on over here." Slocum got one of the older cowboys to join him. "You drove the Bar M herd last year, didn't you?"

"This'll be my third year."

"Anything about the route to the railroad I ought to know?"

"You the trail boss, Slocum? Or you just one of us dust eaters?"

Slocum considered the matter. Magnuson hadn't given him the job, but whenever something had to be done after Blassingame had been laid up, the rancher had told Slocum to do it. He was acting as foreman, even if he hadn't been hired on for that job.

"Don't know what I am," Slocum said. He forced himself to stop thinking about Christine and the square dance that night. "Doesn't much matter since the more all of us know about the trail, the better we'll ride it."

The cowboy scratched his stubbled chin, pushed his hat back, and finally said, "Hashknife's got a map. Can you believe that? He worked for the Army as a scout before gettin' his leg all broke up."

"He ridden the trail before?"

"As often as Blassingame, maybe more. Jed's only been here ten years. Hashknife's born and raised in this country. No idea how long he's worked for Mr. Magnuson but it was 'fore that daughter of his was born."

"Goes back a ways, then," Slocum said. Everything conspired to remind him of Christine. He felt an obligation to do what he could getting the herd to market, but for two cents he would ride back to the ranch house and spirit Christine away. Let Magnuson drag out that old shotgun of his. Slocum was willing to fight for her.

"Hey, Slocum," shouted another cowboy. "We done penned up the downers and chased off the rest. We got ourselves a herd!"

"There's a barn dance tonight, over at the Norton spread. Everybody's invited. Get yourselves cleaned up and in your Sunday best. No blowing off steam, no getting drunk, just a whale of a lot of dancing," Slocum called.

He had no idea if the dance was open to all the hands, but it didn't matter much to him. If Magnuson's entire crew showed up, was Norton going to turn them away? If he tried, there might be some friction between the families. Slocum grinned at that happening. It'd be a shame.

"A damned shame," he muttered. Then he gave the signal for the cowboys to head back to the bunkhouse. One way or the other, it was going to be a memorable night.

The dance was held in a meadow some distance from the Norton barn, but Slocum worried he wasn't dressed well enough for the crowd already gathered. He had been right that Norton hadn't invited any of the cowboys, just the ranchers and their families. But he and Magnuson had gone to one side and talked at length until Norton slapped Magnuson on the shoulder and the two had returned to the festivities.

Whatever agreement had been reached, Magnuson's crew was allowed to remain.

The difference in revelers was quickly apparent to some of Slocum's fellow cowboys. Jonesy came over and expressed his dismay at standing out like tits on a boar hog.

"They're not chasing us off. Go on, dance," Slocum urged. He saw the younger Norton across the meadow joking with several friends. They were all dressed fit to kill. Even Slocum's Sunday best was a poor second to their fancy duds. The more of Magnuson's cowboys that remained, the better Slocum would feel about the quality of his clothing.

"Reckon that means we kin eat the food and drink the punch?"

"You're a guest. Enjoy yourself."

Jonesy let out a whoop of glee and made a beeline for the punch bowl. Slocum doubted it held anything alcoholic but someone hovering near it might have a bottle to add a little nip.

The fiddler struck up a lively song, and the caller bellowed for a Texas Star. Slocum moved around the edge of the crowd watching the dancers, then stopped and watched as Christine danced with Josh Norton. He pushed through the people and waited as the couple swung back past.

Christine never noticed him but Norton did. The young man scowled and then hurried across the ring, swung about, and came back to Christine as the fiddler slowed and finally stopped with a flourish.

Before the next song began, Slocum stepped up, interposed himself between Norton and Christine, and said, "My dance."

"But—"

Slocum ignored Norton's sputtering protests as the fiddler struck up a new tune. He took her in his arms and pulled her closer than was socially acceptable. She tensed and tried to stiffen her arm to push him away. He didn't budge against her pressure.

"You didn't look too put out dancing with him," Slocum said.

"His pa is holding the dance. I had to, John. Really!"

They swung about, separated, and came back together.

"You didn't have to look like you enjoyed it so much."

"Why, John Slocum, you're jealous. There's no need to be."

Slocum started to tell her what he felt, how he wanted to spend the rest of his life with her, when a commotion from the direction of the caller caused the dancers to miss a beat. Some collided; others just stopped and looked.

"That's Hashknife," Christine said. "Looks as if he's got a snootful of booze."

The cook began bellowing out conflicting instructions, then turned to berate the fiddler for not playing loud enough.

"You should stop him before he creates more of a scene," she said.

"Why me?"

"Papa said you were working as foreman with Mr. Blassingame laid up the way he is."

"Not getting paid to be foreman," he said, then realized he was getting off the topic burning brightest in his mind. "Let's get away from here. I want to ask you something—"

"That's your man," the senior Norton said, laying his hand on Slocum's shoulder. "Why not calm him down 'fore some of my men put a bullet in his damn fool head?"

"I have other business."

"Slocum!" This shout came from Mordecai Magnuson. "Get him out of here 'fore I have to fire him."

"Go on, John. We can talk later," Christine said.

Slocum found himself the center of attention, not the drunken cook and his increasingly obscene calls.

"Later," he said. Slocum backed away, brushing off Norton's hand. As he headed for the rowdy cook, the younger Norton returned to speak with Christine. It was less a talk than an argument. That soothed Slocum's ruffled feathers enough to take care of Hashknife.

The cook spun around, using his crippled leg as an axle. One arm waved high in the air and he shouted incoherently now. In the hand not grabbing for the stars, he held a silver flask. Liquor sloshed out as he whirled around and around.

Slocum judged the rotation, stepped forward, and threw both arms around the cook's shoulders. With a grunt, he lifted Hashknife off the ground. His bad leg twitched, and his good one kicked higher in the air.

"You gonna dance with me, Slocum? Didn't know you cared."

"Come on," Slocum said, carrying the cook bodily away from the party. The meadow was demarcated on one side by a swiftly flowing stream. With a heave, Hashknife was added to the leaves and other debris on the frothy surface.

He splashed around in the cold water, sputtered, and tried to sit up. The swift current forced him flat onto his back. His face disappeared under the water. Slocum waded in, grabbed, and pulled the cook up to keep him from drowning.

"You sober enough to go back to the dance?" Slocum shook him like a terrier would a rat.

The cook sputtered and nodded.

"Behave yourself or next time I won't bother pulling you out of the water."

"You're a prince among men, Slocum. A real prince," Hashknife said. Slocum gave him a hand when the cook's bad leg buckled under him. In spite of the dunking, he still smelled of liquor but seemed sober enough for polite company.

Slocum trailed him up the hill to the meadow, where the square dance continued. He looked for Christine but didn't see her. Magnuson and the elder Norton stood close together by the table holding the punch bowl, speaking in animated terms. Magnuson gestured and snippets of Norton's loud voice drifted over the music and general merriment to Slocum's ears. He gritted his teeth and started to hunt for Christine. The two men were talking dowry and marriage.

He would put an end to such talk by convincing Christine to leave with him. They could find the justice of the peace and get hitched right away. That would settle the matter once and for all.

Skirting the edge of the crowd, Slocum hunted for Christine or the younger Norton. If they were still together, all the better. He'd make it clear to the young rancher where things stood.

"Psst. Psst!"

The sound stopped Slocum. A few gnarled trees, one more dead than alive, hid whoever called to him. A shadowy hand reached out and beckoned to him.

"Christine, it's about time you came to your senses." Slocum walked over to have it out.

As he ducked under the limb of the nearly dead tree, a heavy weight fell from above and bore him to the ground. He started to struggle, then found a bag pulled down over his head. Strong hands caught his wrists and he found himself hog-tied as securely as any calf waiting for the branding iron.

9

Slocum gingerly tested the ropes around his wrists. Whoever had tied them had secured him too well to get free. The black bag kept him from seeing where he was taken. From the noises around him, at least three men shepherded him away from the dance. The sounds of the fiddler and the caller faded and soon were completely swallowed by the burbling stream making its way across the meadow. They sloshed through the water and kept walking.

The longer they walked, the more the knot in his belly constricted. He had made his presence known to Junior, who must have ordered some of the cowboys working for his pa to get rid of his competition. Rather than die with a bag over his head, Slocum began straining against the ropes, rubbing his wrists raw, causing blood to flow. When this happened, he knew he had very few minutes to win free. The blood would soak into the hemp strands as it dried, cause the bonds to tighten.

But for a short while it made his wrists slippery enough to work free of the constricting loops of rope. He staggered and went to one knee when his hands came free.

Silent hands pulled him back to his feet and shoved him along. It took all his willpower not to swing around, strike out, and try to break free. From the footsteps, he was pretty sure there were only three. He could punch out one on his left, swing around using the rope as a whip, and lash another across the face. The third one—the one trailing them by a few paces—would be the most difficult. He'd have to rip off the bag before dealing with the last captor.

"You are an amazing fellow, Slocum," came a voice he recognized. "Why don't you go on and pull off that black sack we got your head stuffed into. I know you got your hands free."

Slocum grabbed a handful of the cloth and yanked. In the dim light he saw Wiley Pendergast sitting on a stump, cleaning his fingernails with a knife. The outlaw pointed the tip at him and nodded approvingly.

"Yes, sir, you are a marvel. Herman there, the one behind you, is about the best I ever did see tyin' up folks. He can throw a calf and get it ready for brandin' in five seconds flat. Don't take half that for a human being. Does it, Herman?"

"Naw, boss. This one was even quicker 'n that. Real easy."

"He can truss you up again, if I tell him."

From the corners of his eyes Slocum saw the men on his flanks. They had stepped away a pace, making it more difficult to reach one and then turn on the other. Both kept hands resting on the butts of their six-shooters. A glance over his shoulder at Herman convinced him he wouldn't be tied up if he tried to escape. He would be dead.

As dead as he'd thought he would have been with Josh Norton kidnapping him from the dance.

"What do you want?" Slocum asked. "If you wanted a dance, this is the wrong place. You can't hear the music this far away."

Pendergast paused a moment, surprise on his face. Then he laughed heartily.

"You are a caution, Slocum. Never doing what I expect. That's what I want from you."

Slocum's mind raced. All of Magnuson's cowboys were at the square dance, leaving the ranch empty. Blassingame was still in bed, but he was so bunged up he wouldn't be able to fight off a mosquito, much less a gang of rustlers.

"You want me to help you rustle the cattle."

"Now that's a fine idea. It shows you aren't simply mooning around after that Magnuson bitch but are working on more important matters."

Slocum tried not to betray his seething emotions. This was worse than playing four professional gamblers and finding a royal flush in his hand. The slightest hint of emotion would ruin him. The difference was profound, though. The worst that could happen if he betrayed his hand was not win much money. Christine would be used as a lever to force him to do what the outlaw leader wanted if he played this hand wrong.

"I won't help you steal the beeves."

"A hint of honesty running through that crooked body of yours? I do declare. This is a new John Slocum I'm talking to. The one I knew robbed trains and stagecoaches and rustled a cow or two when the opportunity presented itself. You remember that, John Slocum? The old one?" Pendergast stood and stepped closer as if examining a bug under a magnifying glass.

"Looks like the same old John Slocum to me. Might be you just need some convincing."

"I won't steal the cattle for you."

"Well, good," Pendergast said unexpectedly. "I don't want you to go near those beeves, not until your boss tells you."

Slocum eyed Pendergast, trying to figure him out. He decided saying nothing benefitted him most until the outlaw showed more of his cards. Whatever game Pendergast played, he was enjoying it. That meant he held all the high cards. Slocum had to let him lay them down to find out what this was all about.

"What's worth more than a few head of cattle?" Pendergast asked.

Slocum refused to be baited and remained silent.

"Why, I'm sure you would agree that it's a whole damned herd of cattle. But what's worth more 'n that? Four herd of cattle."

"You're going to rustle all the ranchers' herds?" Then Slocum turned what he'd said around. That was absurd. It would take a hundred men, maybe more, to pull off such a crime. And what would Pendergast do with thousands of head of cattle? Driving them across the prairie would leave a swath a blind man could follow—and follow it the ranchers would. With blood in their eye, with six-shooters cocked, and with nooses tied.

There was something else Pendergast might mean, and it was even more audacious than Slocum had thought possible to be cooked up in the outlaw's fertile imagination. He sucked in his breath. Such audacity!

"Ah, you are quick on the uptake, Slocum. Let the ranchers sell their herds, stuff all that money in their pockets—for a few days."

"They'll put the money in the bank."

"Four huge herds ought to bring in tens of thousands of dollars. I've checked and the bills the ranchers have racked up will be paid out of the proceeds. And where do the merchants keep their money? In the same lonely bank."

"I have to hand it to you, Pendergast. That's mighty clever."

The outlaw motioned. Herman brought around a horse.

"Mount up. We're going into town. We can be the first customers."

Slocum bit back the question. The herds were a week or more from being sold. Why rob the bank now?

They rode in silence. Slocum counted six others with Pendergast. Trying to get away, especially in the dark, would be difficult. A horse galloping across the prairie stood a good chance of stepping into a prairie dog hole and breaking a leg. As long they remained on the road going into town, Slocum knew he could never sneak away. There simply wasn't anywhere he could dodge and hope to get out of sight long enough to confound Pendergast and his gang.

It was just after dawn when they rode into town. Pendergast gave quiet orders to his men. Only Herman remained with him and Slocum as they rode to the bank and waited silently for a teller to open the front door.

"Top of the morning to you, sir. Is your president in yet?"

"He is, sir. Mr. Roebuck's not one to let the grass grow under his feet."

The teller held the door for them as the three entered.

Pendergast took Slocum by the arm and held him back.

"Check the vault, see what it'll take to open it."

"You mean blow it open?"

"A lot depends on how we rob the bank in a couple weeks. Do we come in with guns blazing and kill the lot of them, or do we break in and open the safe in the middle of the night? You're the expert on blasting, Slocum. I heard stories of how you—"

"May I help you gents?" The bank president hooked his thumbs in the armholes of his fancy silver brocade vest. A long gold chain dangled across the front to vanish into a pocket, where Slocum suspected an equally expensive watch was tucked away. Roebuck was tall, thin as a rail, and wore muttonchops that carried just a hint of gray. His eyes took in Herman and dismissed him right away. They lingered on Pendergast but fixed on Slocum.

"You, you're one of Mr. Magnuson's boys, aren't you?"

"He is," Pendergast said, speaking for Slocum. "We're here to reassure Mordecai that your bank's secure."

"What's that? Mr. Magnuson's been a good customer of the First State Bank for more than twenty years! He can't think to move his account elsewhere!"

"He doesn't want to," Pendergast said smoothly. "He just wants to be assured that his money is safe in your vault."

"Of course it is!"

"Could we see?" Pendergast poked Slocum in the ribs and pushed him forward. "Mr. Slocum here's taking over for Jed while he's laid up."

Slocum was irritated at how well Pendergast knew the Bar M Ranch's business. He had to have poked around finding out the names and everything that was going on for some time. Still, if a robber wanted to pull off a successful bank theft, attention to detail was vital.

What galled Slocum most was how Pendergast used him as a pawn. Roebuck might not remember Herman or Pendergast, but he would remember Slocum being one of Magnuson's employees. If Pendergast was successful robbing the bank, Slocum was implicated. He reluctantly appreciated how the outlaw had maneuvered him. It no longer mattered if he took part in the robbery. He was going to be accused.

Turbulent thoughts boiled about in his head. Christine and Josh Norton. Being identified as one of the men with Pendergast, and Pendergast was sure to let it be known he robbed the bank. His arrogance knew no bounds. He would think of that as an artist signing his painting.

Killing Pendergast didn't seem easy. Slocum rubbed his hands on his hips. He was dressed in his finery, such as it was, and hadn't worn a six-gun. Even killing the outlaw later wouldn't be much good. Herman or the others would turn him over to the marshal, and standing beside Pendergast here and now damned him.

"I'm not sure what it is you want to see," Roebuck said, frowning. "Mr. Slocum? What is it you do for Mr. Magnuson?"

"You might say he's Mordecai's agent. All we need to do is look around. Don't even have to go into the vault, if that's against bank rules," Pendergast said smoothly. "There can't be any harm in that, can there? Reassuring Mr. Magnuson that his money will be nice and safe in your vault."

"I suppose not." Roebuck shot a look at his two tellers. Both men reached under the counter, going for six-shooters hidden there.

"Excellent!" Pendergast slapped the banker on the back and made his own way toward the vault at the rear of the bank. The door stood open, and the inside of the vault was cloaked in darkness.

Slocum took in the details of the door. It would take more nitroglycerin than Pendergast was likely to come by to blow the heavy steel door off its hinges. Locking bars seated in the heavy jamb in three places. He could not tell but thought there were three more locking bars on the hinge side. For smaller safes, the front could be peeled back like skinning a deer to reveal the innards. This vault door was too sturdy for that.

He took as long a look around inside as he could, then turned and smiled.

"I'll report back to Mr. Magnuson that your vault is as secure as any I have seen."

"You're an expert in these matters, Mr. Slocum?"

"None better," Pendergast said, slapping Slocum on the back. His fingers dug into his shoulder and steered him away from the vault. "Much obliged for your time, Mr. Roebuck."

Outside, the sun had risen fully above the horizon. The day was going to be a hot one. Slocum worked to loosen his collar.

"So what do we need to break in?" Pendergast said. He tipped his hat to a passing woman, who favored him with a quick, shy smile before hurrying on. The outlaw ran his finger around the snakeskin band on the hat, reset the angle to something jauntier, then pointed.

"Walk around the bank," Slocum said.

They stopped near a pile of debris. Slocum's expert

appraisal located the precise point where the vault wall was weakest. He leaned against the brick.

"Blow through here. You're going to need a couple cases of dynamite. Drill holes a foot apart all over this area, set it off, and you're inside."

"No way of getting through that vault door, is there? Never laid eyes on anything that solid."

"If you don't like the idea of blowing down the wall, you can always tunnel in, but I saw some bolts along one wall. Roebuck might have laid down a steel plate to keep out varmints."

"To keep out varmints," Pendergast said, laughing. "You are a funny man, Slocum. We're going to be rich, the lot of us." He turned and walked away.

"Wait a minute," Slocum called. "Leave me a horse."

"You'll be rich enough to buy one of your own soon enough," Pendergast said. The easy smile carried a hint of cruelty now. If Slocum hadn't known before, he did now. The bank would be robbed, and John Slocum would either be left with a bullet in his head or otherwise set up as scapegoat. Everything Pendergast had done today worked toward indelibly tying Slocum into the robbery.

The outlaws rode away in a cloud of dust. Slocum brushed off the dirt as it settled, wondering how far he would get going straight to the marshal. If he tried that, the lawman would think the outlaws had had a falling-out and arrest him. Slocum didn't want the marshal pawing through a stack of wanted posters. Other than the judge killing, he had a few others with rewards sizable enough to portray him as a desperado.

It was a long walk back to the Bar M but he decided, since he was already in town, he would see how Tom Garvin fared. It didn't surprise him that Dr. Abbey was already in his office. With a patient as seriously injured as Garvin, he would want to keep a close eye on him.

He pushed the door open and poked his head in. For a

moment, he wasn't sure what he was seeing. Then he blurted out, "Garvin!"

The young man turned. He spun his rope, doing tricks. The loop danced and sang as he agilely stepped in and out of the spinning circle. With a flourish he widened the loop and lifted it up off the floor. He stood in the middle of the whirl, then let it drop.

"Gets me tuckered out faster 'n I'd like," he said, gathering the black rope and curling it into a large loop he held in his left hand.

"You were half past dead when I brought you in. You shouldn't be able to sit up, much less twirl a lariat like that. You're doing tricks nobody does outside a Wild West Show."

"Do tell," Garvin said. He dropped onto the table where the doctor had extracted the bullet from his body. Garvin idly scratched the spot, now covered with a small patch of snow white bandage.

"Remarkable recovery," Dr. Abbey said, coming from an inner room. "Never seen anything like it. Wish I could take credit but I can't."

"If you had more patients like me, you'd have to find another profession," Garvin joked.

"If I had more patients like you, the undertaker'd be out of business in a month."

"You come to pick me up, Slocum? I'm rarin' to git on back to work."

"I . . ." Slocum gathered his thoughts. "I'm on foot. Left my horse at the square dance last night."

"Big times, eh?" Abbey looked at him with a bit of envy in his expression. "To be young and foolish again." He poked and probed Garvin, then added, "To be young and able to heal like that again. You get on out of here. I've got to see real patients."

"No offense, Doc, but in spite of the good job you did patchin' me up, I don't want to see you again."

"No offense taken. Now go, go!" Dr. Abbey began putting

the supplies he had fetched from the back room into a glass-fronted cabinet.

"You weren't joshin' that you were on foot. If we want to get back to the ranch before sundown, we'd better start hikin'."

Slocum stared at Tom Garvin's back as the young man set out for the Bar M on foot. No one would have believed he had shot himself in the chest from the strong, long stride and the way he uncurled his rope and began doing fancy tricks with it as he went.

Slower, Slocum began the walk back to the ranch, too, not knowing what he would find when he got there.

10

"It ain't fair!"

Slocum had no time to deal with Tom Garvin's petty wailing.

"You're lucky Magnuson let you ride along as Hash-knife's helper. You're not strong enough to put in a day's work, not in the saddle, not with riding picket at night."

"I am, too," Garvin complained. "It wasn't that bad a wound." He pounded his chest to make his point. Slocum saw the boy wince.

And he winced at the sight of the S&W swinging at Garvin's hip. He should have learned something trying to clean the gun and accidentally shooting himself. Only pure luck had saved his life. Slocum had seen men with a bullet through the heart drop as if all the bones in their legs had turned to jelly. Garvin being on the trail drive was nothing less than a miracle.

"Everybody on the drive shares in the bonus," Slocum said. "What you're doing is more important than any of us."

"What do you mean?" Garvin fingered his black rope and looked suspicious.

"You've got to keep Hashknife from poisoning us. I swear, I never rode with a worse cook. Those biscuits he made this morning were so hard I chipped a tooth."

"They weren't so good, huh?" Garvin looked rueful. "I kin cook better, and I'm awful at it. All he has me doin' is cleanin' them damned pots when he burns the food to the bottoms."

"Too bad," Slocum said. "The grease is about the only thing that gives taste to the food. You do as he says. You'll be back in shape by next season, and then you won't be the tenderfoot."

"I'm no greenhorn, not now! I—"

Slocum rode away. He didn't have any more time for Garvin. Jonesy said the cattle were a bit skittish from a pack of wolves running parallel to the trail. This was the best time of year for the gray killers. Food was brought to them.

He rode to the far edge of the herd and found Jonesy with a rifle out and laid across his saddle.

"Don't go taking any potshots," Slocum warned. "You'll start a stampede for sure."

"The wolf pack might do that anyway." He pointed to a low rise. Outlined against the blue sky were three of the predators. Slocum could almost hear the wolves licking their chops as they studied the herd for the weakest, the slowest, the ones that provided the best chance for a full lupine belly.

"Any sign of rustlers?"

Jonesy looked at him sharply.

"Just making sure, that's all." Even to Slocum the words rang hollow.

"You don't seem the type to get all riled. Did them rustlers spook you? Back in the canyon when Blassingame got all shot up?"

"We recovered two-dozen head for Magnuson," Slocum said obliquely. He wasn't worried about being in a gunfight with Wiley Pendergast and the rest of his gang. His concern ran deeper, but he couldn't tell the cowboy that. Of the riders working the herd, he trusted Jonesy most. And Slocum was hardly going to share more than his thoughts about the herd and the cowboys working it.

Jonesy shrugged it off.

"Want me to ride over and chase them off?" Five gray wolves now lined the ridge, spectators in a deadly game that might cost the Bar M hundreds of dollars.

"Keep to the trail. I'll do some scouting."

Slocum snapped the reins on his horse and trotted toward the ridge. The wolves sank back behind the crest. By the time he rode the ridge, they were nowhere to be found. He dismounted and studied the tracks. One paw print was bigger than the palm of his hand. These weren't just big wolves; they were huge. A wolf needed a deer a week to stay alive. A pack this size—and Slocum tried to sort through the jumble of prints—might number eight or ten. For the week they were on the trail, the pack might take a dozen steers.

He considered decoying them away with a sickly cow or two, but he knew such appeasement never worked. If anything, leaving behind a sacrificial steer would only embolden the wolves and convince them even more food was available. He touched the Colt Navy slung in its cross-draw holster and knew what sort of deterrent was required. A dead wolf or two would chase off the rest. They weren't stupid animals, and if it looked as if the entire pack would be hunted and killed, they would go after easier pickings.

Let them eat the entire damned Norton herd, for all Slocum cared.

The thought of Norton and his son set off a new train of thought that he didn't much like. There hadn't been any time to talk with Christine after he and Garvin had hoofed it all the way back to the ranch from town. Magnuson had kept them mighty busy for the next two days preparing their gear and being sure the herd was well fed and watered. The stronger the cattle started the drive, the more hardship they could endure on the trail.

Slocum reckoned the hazards for the Bar M drive were less lack of water and grass and more like the gray wolves. And the two-legged ones led by Pendergast.

From the ridge he saw how Jonesy drove the cattle down into a ravine, making sure they kept moving but without rushing them. It took only one frightened steer to start the tide of beef moving inexorably. Slocum had never seen a stampede that didn't end with dozens of cattle being killed, and sometimes almost as many cowboys.

He considered going after the wolves and trying to bring down one or two. Skinned as a warning and left for the buzzards, dead wolves served a purpose. But he was still too close to the herd to risk a rifle shot. For more than fifteen minutes he followed the wolf tracks and then lost them on a rocky patch.

It didn't take any genius to figure where the wolves had gone, but Slocum wasn't inclined to pursue them. He rode alongside the herd, watching Jonesy and the others keep the herd together as they came out of the mile-long ravine. Turning his attention more to rustlers than four-legged cattle thieves, he scanned the horizon for any trace of Pendergast and his outlaws. He might as well have been alone on the range.

In spite of Pendergast saying he intended to rob the bank after the drive had brought in a year's worth of money, Slocum knew better than to take anything the outlaw said at face value. Pendergast was a thinker, always scheming, always looking for the angle to play. If he could steal a few cattle along the way, that might tickle his fancy. He had been willing to rob Magnuson of a couple dozen head not a week earlier. The owlhoot's change of mind could have come from the revelation of how much more he could steal—and how much easier it would be. Or it could be a ruse. With Pendergast, he never knew until the six-gun cleared the holster and gun smoke filled the air.

Slocum wondered if he should have gone back to the

bank and told Roebuck to strengthen the wall, to hire extra guards, to be especially alert for a robbery. The way Pendergast had lassoed him and brought him into the scheme, it might not have worked. Roebuck might have seen any warning as proof positive Slocum was intent on robbing the bank.

An hour of lonely scouting took him back to the herd. He shouted, got a few recalcitrant steers moving with the others, then rode to where Jonesy argued with Tom Garvin. The young man sat astride one of the spare horses from the remuda.

"I'm able. I kin do it, Jonesy. Don't go gettin' all—"

"Garvin." Slocum spoke his name with such coldness that both Tom Garvin and Jonesy looked around, hands going to their sidearms. "I want a word with you."

"I wanna talk to you, too, Slocum. This yahoo—"

"Now."

They rode twenty yards to the side of the herd.

"I kin do it, John. I swear it. I'm not some hothouse flower that needs to be pampered."

"Not saying you are, but Mr. Magnuson gave orders. You ride with the chuck wagon, not with the cattle."

"Why have me along if you're not gonna let me work?" Garvin's belligerence grew to the point that Slocum wondered if anger would drive the youngster into throwing down. One hand moved restlessly along the silver threads in the black rope. The other slipped back and forth on the holster at his side.

If Garvin tried to draw, it would be the last thing he ever did. Slocum was a crack shot, but facing a man as wild as Garvin was always dangerous. He couldn't control his sixgun, and he sure as hell wasn't much of a marksman. That made him too unsafe to tolerate. He might get off a round and shoot another cowboy.

Worse, he could start a stampede and kill the lot of them.

"I'm not the foreman. Hell, I don't even know if I'm the trail boss, but I'm acting like one. Until Magnuson tells me different, I do what he says. And he said you weren't to sit astride that horse of yours."

"How kin I hold my head up if you treat me as a kid?"

"You think Hashknife is a kid because he's cook?"

"Naw, but he's all crippled up. That busted leg of his keeps him from ridin'."

"Your bullet wound needs time to heal, no matter what you think. Dr. Abbey said so and Magnuson agreed." Slocum took a deep breath as he studied Garvin for further rebellion. Sending him back to the Bar M wasn't something he hankered to do, but he would. Discord on the trail only added to everyone's stress. This was dangerous enough a job without a young snot like Tom Garvin adding to it.

"What makes you the one to decide?" Garvin thrust out his chin, begging Slocum to land a quick left jab on it. If they had been closer, he would have been tempted.

"You got a point there," Slocum admitted. "Blassingame isn't here and Magnuson has gone on to the railhead to begin negotiating for the herd. The other cowboys sort of put me in charge. That's not something I asked for."

"That's not somethin' I go along with either," Garvin said.

"Take it up with Mr. Magnuson." Slocum wished Garvin would ride ahead and have it out with the rancher. That would get him out of his hair and let him deal with the work at hand. Driving a herd of cattle, even only a hundred miles, was a chore that required all his attention. He was carrying a load of responsibility without being given the authority.

"You—" Garvin gritted his teeth, then wheeled his horse around and rode away. Slocum wondered where he was going.

It was too much to hope that Garvin actually went to put his complaint in front of the rancher.

Slocum trotted back to the edge of the herd, keeping stragglers moving along until midday. He waved to Jonesy and called, "Time to get some grub. Have three hands watch the herd while the rest of us eat."

Jonesy acknowledged with a wave. Slocum's belly grumbled so loud that his horse turned and stared at him, one huge brown eye questioning the sound.

"You can crop some grass. Looks tasty here," Slocum said, patting the horse's neck. He had been sorry to lose his mare to the rustlers, but this one was sturdy and had heart.

"Hashknife," he called. "Get your witch's stew ready. You got hungry riders coming in."

The cook hopped around, then dropped a big iron pot and cursed. Whatever was in the pot sloshed out.

"Damnation, that was your share o' the food, Slocum. You're gonna hafta go hungry awhile longer."

"You might have saved my life letting you poison the others first." Slocum dropped to the ground and went to help the cook. Only a small amount of the vile-smelling stew had spilled. Slocum caught up the wire handle and heaved. Hashknife had a small cooking fire crackling. With a grunt, Slocum dropped the handle onto the wire hook dangling from a tripod over the fire.

"Thank you kindly," the cook said. "You helpin' me with the rest of the meal?"

"Where's Garvin?"

"Ain't seen that varmint. He lit out 'bout an hour back. I figgered you fired him for bein' such a layabout."

Slocum considered doing just that, but he had other problems. He helped the cook get the food ready. Six cowboys rode in and chowed down, left, and then Jonesy and the remaining three settled down to plates of the stew.

"I know I been on the trail too long," Jonesy said. "This tastes good."

"You've only been on the trail for five hours," Slocum said, checking his pocket watch.

"By supper you'll be ready to eat your own boots, and do I have a dandy recipe for 'em!" Hashknife laughed. Jonesy made a face, then continued scooping up the stew.

Slocum looked over the herd and saw how the cattle were becoming restless.

"Jonesy, you see those wolves again?"

"Nope. Been on the lookout but ain't even seen a rabbit, not that that's so strange. They feel the ground shakin' from the cattle."

"There's something wrong. Mount up. All of you."

"What's wrong? Don't see nuthin'." Jonesy stood on tiptoe and craned his neck. "You gettin' the second sight, Slocum?"

He had worked on enough trail drives to have the uneasy feeling when something bad was about to happen. Slocum vaulted into the saddle and headed for the front of the herd. As he rode, he heard lowing, as if a cow was in pain. Homing in on the anguished sound, he found his path quickly blocked by milling cattle.

"What's wrong?" Jonesy shouted. "I don't see nuthin', Slocum."

"There, to the side of the herd. Something's riling them up over there." Slocum put his heels to his horse's flanks and forced his way through the nearest knot of cattle.

If a steer had broken a leg in a prairie dog hole, its cries would frighten the rest of the herd. Slocum grabbed the loop of rope at his knee and swung it to swat cattle out of his way. The herd parted reluctantly. He felt the tension mounting through the herd that stretched to the horizon. The only lucky thing was finally getting the herd out of the deep ravine they had entered early in the morning. That constriction would have caused the cattle to climb over one another in their panic.

The closer Slocum got to the bellowing steer, the colder he felt in his gut. He saw a cow with a leg caught, but he also saw the crown of a cowboy's hat bobbing about. Somebody had dismounted and tried to free the steer from whatever had entangled it.

"Get onto your horse. Mount up!" he shouted and knew

his words were muffled under the deepening thunder as the herd began moving.

He got closer and saw Tom Garvin on his knees, trying to pull the steer's hoof from between two rocks where it had trapped itself.

"Leave the cow. Get the hell out of the way!"

Garvin looked up. His expression carried nothing but disdain. And then it changed to fear when it became obvious what was happening.

Stampede. And he was directly in front of the herd.

11

Slocum yelled as he rode. The pounding of hooves grew all around him as he put his head down and raked his horse's flanks with his spurs to get the most speed possible.

"Garvin, dammit, Garvin! Let the steer be!"

Tom Garvin stared past Slocum at the surging tide of frightened cattle. He opened his mouth to speak, then clamped it shut. Something broke him free of his shock, and he reached for the reins of his horse.

The steer he had been trying to free broke away. From the way it stumbled along, it had hurt its leg. It crashed into Garvin's horse and spooked it. The horse bolted, causing the cowboy to grab wildly for the saddle horn.

His fingers caught the pommel and slipped away. As he fell facedown, his hand tangled in the black rope. His horse spun and lashed out with its front hooves. It knocked off his hat, but Garvin hung on to the rope. Without it, his horse would have run away, dooming him.

Slocum saw everything moving in slow motion. Garvin got to his feet, only to make another mistake. He purposefully unfastened his rope from the saddle, letting the horse rocket off. Garvin took a couple steps and fell to his knees, clutching his rope and nothing else.

Bending low, Slocum reached down and grabbed for Garvin. He caught the cowboy's shirt and yanked him to his feet.

"Climb on behind me," Slocum grated out. He was panting harshly, as if he had run a mile. He jerked hard on Garvin's hand and lifted him to the rear of his horse. He wasted no time seeing if Garvin was settled. He got his horse running at an angle, thinking to avoid the worst of the stampede and let the cattle rush past.

It didn't work that way.

The extra weight caused his horse to falter. Slocum kept trying to get it turned, but the horse kept jerking in the direction of the worst danger—smack in front of the running cattle.

"We can't outrun 'em," Garvin said, hanging on to Slocum.

The feel of the young man's arms gave Slocum something more to worry over. Garvin weakened and wobbled. Whether it came from his brush with death or the chest wound had finally caught up with him didn't matter. He might fall to his death at any instant.

"Hang on tighter," Slocum shouted. His words were swallowed by the roar of the cattle.

If his horse wouldn't turn, he had to give it its head and try to outrun the steers. One polled horn hooked Slocum's leg and almost yanked him from horseback. He steadied himself and saw the only hope to survive. Hashknife waved from atop the chuck wagon. This was the only possible island of safety in a sea of terrified beeves.

He heard Garvin shout something but paid no attention. Slocum focused on the chuck wagon, on Hashknife giving him what little directions he could to reach it. Within fifty yards, his horse died under him. Slocum felt the animal stiffen, then turn to liquid. He flew ass over teakettle and landed flat on his back, staring up at the sky.

A strong hand pulled him up.

"Come on, Slocum. We gotta run. The cattle!"

He saw a frightened Tom Garvin waving his rope about, as if this could brush off the full fury of a stampede. Without answering, he started running. Hashknife started to come out to help.

"Go back, we can make it, go back!"

Slocum's words were drowned out. The cook hobbled out to help. And then the lead steer bumped Slocum and sent him flying. Slocum sailed past Hashknife and skidded on his belly beneath the chuck wagon.

"Help!"

Hashknife's cry didn't go unheeded. Garvin spun his rope and let it sail out in a broad loop. It came down over the cook's body. Garvin started pulling. Slocum got to his feet and went to help, but he knew what happened an instant later. Garvin fell backward and sat down, no resistance on the rope.

Hashknife had been trampled to death.

"He—"

Slocum shoved Garvin along in the dust to a spot just beyond the chuck wagon. The stampeding cattle crashed into the wagon and knocked it over. Slocum had judged just right. The chuck wagon fell onto its side and sent a cascade of food and supplies through the air. Slocum threw up an arm to protect his head from the rain, shoved Garvin back toward the wagon and then slid so his back was pressed against the wagon bed.

"What?" Garvin started to run when the entire wagon shook hard.

"Stay put," Slocum said. "We might get out of this alive if we use the wagon as a shield."

"Hashknife, he was trampled."

"Dead," Slocum said harshly. He wanted to break Garvin out of his shock and have him start thinking about ways to stay alive.

The impact of one heavy cow after another on the far

side of the chuck wagon began to take its toll. Nails popped free. Wood planks splintered. The entire wagon was moved foot after foot every time a steer rammed headlong into it. Slocum hunched up, as if this would make him a smaller target. Mostly he wanted this nightmare to be done. Once he had survived a stampede by shooting the lead cow and using its carcass as a shield. He had been badly cut up and shaken by the experience, but he had come out alive.

He could survive again.

Garvin held his rope in slack hands, staring at it. The silver thread caught the sunlight and somehow formed a beacon through the din and dust kicked up by the stampede.

"I had him. I shoulda saved him."

The roar of hooves slowly died away, and after an eternity Slocum saw the last of the cattle pass the sanctuary of the overturned wagon.

"They're not runnin' no more. They're just walkin'." Garvin sounded outraged.

"They ran along because the others were. The cattle at the rear of the herd weren't as scared, didn't have any reason to run other 'n the others were, too." Slocum stood and brushed off the thick layer of dust on his clothing. He created a brand-new dust storm and sneezed as it tickled his nose. Spitting, he got the grit from his tongue. A nearby canteen helped wash even more from his mouth so he didn't bite down on sand.

"That don't make sense."

Slocum didn't ask what didn't make any sense. Garvin was still in a daze.

Walking around the wagon allowed him to see the real damage. Hashknife had been trampled to the point that he was only recognizable by his dirty apron. Here and there a few head had suffered the same fate, but there weren't as many dead cattle as Slocum had anticipated.

"I never seen nuthin' like that," Garvin said, his voice shaky.

Slocum heard a hissing sound and glanced over his shoulder. Garvin spun the rope, not even knowing he did so.

"Find a shovel," Slocum said. "We got some digging to do."

He heard Garvin puking out his guts. He didn't blame the tenderfoot. Seeing a man stomped to death by a herd of cattle wasn't something to get over easily. Slocum went and pawed through the debris left from the chuck wagon, wondering as he did so how they were going to finish the drive. Maybe if they divvied up the food among all the riders, they could reach the railhead without having to live off the land. Shooting dinner was bad on a couple scores. The rifle shots would spook the herd and it took a fair amount of time to track down and kill even a rabbit. Better to make as quick a trip of it as possible.

They could always slaughter a cow a day, but without the chuck wagon to carry what they didn't eat, that meant they'd have to butcher a cow for every meal. That took time and Slocum doubted Magnuson would be overly pleased.

He found a small shovel and went to where Hashknife had been killed. Garvin stood over the body, staring down with wide eyes.

"Th-there, over there," he said, pointing to a spot between a couple low-growing bushes. "I think Hashknife would like there."

Slocum doubted the cook cared one whit now, but he went, stuck the shovel into the ground, and found the digging easy enough. It took the better part of an hour to finish the grave. By the time he finished, Jonesy had come up with two others.

"Reckon we're lucky," Jonesy said. "Only Hashknife got himself kilt. Everyone else got out of the way."

"I'll bury him, then you and the others take everything you can from the supplies. That wagon's not going to roll another inch."

"Don't know what happened to the team, neither," Jonesy

said. "Might be all the way to Saint Louis by now, if they ever stop runnin'."

"Should we say something over him?" Garvin asked as Slocum and Jonesy dragged the blanket-wrapped body to the grave.

"Say whatever suits you," Slocum said. He had been to too many funerals for the words to carry any real meaning for him. There might be a promised land and it might be better than this world, but he found himself more worried about staying where he was. Fine words and heaven were too alien for him to understand or appreciate after all the men he had known who had died violently or even in bed with their boots off.

"We got every crate and sack divided into parcels. I'll get the boys to come by and each take one," said Jonesy. "What more do you want us to do, Slocum?"

Again Slocum found himself faced with being looked up to as the trail boss. They expected him to know what to do.

"The cattle are all tuckered out. Bed 'em down early while we still got sunlight. At the crack of dawn we ought to be on the trail again."

"I kin use a bit of rest myself," Jonesy said. "And you need to fix yourself up, too, Slocum."

"What do you mean?"

"Your leg's all tore up," Garvin said. "I kin do some bandagin'. I seen how Dr. Abbey worked." He smiled ruefully. "My time in the doc's office ought to have been for some worthwhile end."

Slocum felt a dull ache in his left leg, then remembered the steer that had batted up against him. The horn, though it had been robbed of its sharp tip, had torn open some skin. Somewhere during the stampede the wound had clotted over, but walking now presented a chore he was hardly up for.

"I'll need a horse. Garvin, too. Both of ours were killed."

"The boys'll keep an eye out. You rest up here a spell, Slocum, and we'll take care of everything."

Jonesy rode off, leaving Slocum and Garvin at the wrecked wagon.

"Found some of this here iodine in Hashknife's supplies. Get that boot off and cut open your pant leg so's I kin dab some on."

Slocum leaned back and closed his eyes. The pain was bearable. He had experienced far worse in his day, but he found it hard to remember when or why. Before he knew it, he drifted off to a fitful sleep, only to come awake with a start when the sound of approaching horses filled his ears.

"We got ourselves some horses, Slocum," Garvin said.

Slocum glumly agreed. These were the scrubs from the remuda, now scattered across the prairie. Still, even the worst of the Bar M horses was better than walking. He had done that too often recently.

"Let's find what happened to our horses," he said.

"Why?" Garvin looked confused. He idly spun the black rope around and around, as if this was all he needed.

"Our gear. The horses are dead, but the saddlebags likely escaped too much damage. And riding bareback doesn't suit me."

"Could be, could be," Garvin said. He smiled. "Let's mount and ride!"

"You ride bareback?" Slocum looked at the horses Jonesy had brought. Definitely horses from the remuda.

"I kin do what I have to," Garvin said with more confidence than Slocum had.

Jonesy passed over the horses. Slocum thanked him for rounding up the two and said, "Got the outriders posted?"

"Surely do, and even set up a rotation. I don't think it's a good idea to let the shifts go more 'n a couple hours."

"Everyone's kinda nervy," Garvin said, nodding. "You got a good head on yer shoulders, Jonesy."

Jonesy ignored the young cowboy and said to Slocum, "What else you want? Help findin' your gear?"

"That's what Slocum said we'd need to do," Garvin said.

When neither of the others paid him any attention, he subsided, grumbling to himself.

"I don't think we'll have to hunt too far," Slocum said. "You tend the herd. I'll be back as soon as I can."

"If you're back 'fore dawn, that'll suit us," Jonesy said.

Slocum knew what the cowboy meant. Again he was being acknowledged as the trail boss. He had considered just riding away when he retrieved his gear, but Jonesy's confidence in him kept him from doing that. And he had business to settle with Christine after the drive. If Magnuson officially promoted him to foreman, this might put him in a better position to ask for Christine's hand in marriage.

"What's on your mind, Slocum?"

"Nothing," he said to Garvin. It irked him that the cowboy got any hint of what was going on outside the drive. One was business, the other was personal. Slocum kept the personal as private as he could.

He vaulted onto the horse, gathered the bridle, and started back to where he had last seen his horse. Garvin trailed silently, having figured out Slocum didn't want idle conversation.

Slocum circled the area. He found what remained of his horse farther from where the chuck wagon had been demolished than he would have thought possible. He slipped from his mount and got to work dragging out his saddle from the dead horse's carcass. He finally held up his saddlebags, glad to have this little of his gear still in one piece.

Without a word to Garvin, he saddled the horse from the remuda—his horse now—and slung the saddlebags. He stepped up and looked around.

"Your horse set off in that direction," Slocum said, pointing toward a low hill. "Let's see if we can find it."

"This one suits me," Garvin said.

"I want to look around. If we find another horse, it's to all our benefit. We don't want to ride our horses into the ground."

"That'd slow us down, that's for certain sure," Garvin said. "Let's go."

Slocum let his horse walk. The ground was chopped up until they reached the foot of the hill. The herd had flowed around the contours and hadn't tried running uphill. If it had, the stampede would have been over in a few minutes. The slope was greater than it looked and Slocum found his mount straining.

He dismounted to walk the horse, then stopped and looked at the ground.

"Find something, Slocum?" Garvin trailed him a couple dozen yards.

"Shod horse came this way." Slocum scowled. From the way the hoofprint had been pressed into the soft earth, there had to be a second horse on the same trail, finding footing in the same spots. He ran his finger around the edge of the hoofprint. The edge of dirt furrow crumbled easily. The tracks were recent. Any wind or rain would have begun erasing the print otherwise.

"Then let's go get it," Garvin said.

"There's no hurry." Slocum held back telling what he had discovered, and he didn't know why. Perhaps the young cowboy proved increasingly arrogant for no good reason. Slocum had seen men who deserved to boast of their deeds and never once took an occasion to do so.

Most of those who had gone through the war were like that. The ones doing the most boasting either had not seen that much action or were like William Quantrill and could never shut up about the men they had killed. Then there were some who bragged on what they had done and were lying through their teeth. Slocum got the feeling that Tom Garvin would turn into one of those if he didn't set himself on the right path soon.

"You're lookin' fer somethin', ain't you, Slocum?"

Whatever else Garvin might be, he wasn't slow to understand what went on around him.

"Several riders, not just one horse."

"Ain't seen nobody ridin' along this ridge, but then I was busy with the stampede."

"That might have sent them to the top of the ridge. That'd be the smart thing to do to get away from the herd," Slocum said. He kept walking until he crested the rise and got a good look all around.

The riders had gone along the ridge, paralleling the direction taken by the herd. That wasn't too suspicious if they had come along after the stampede started. Otherwise, travelers might just stop by and invite themselves for dinner. No trail cook was going to pass up the chance to serve a juicy steak to both the trail hands and visitors. Ranchers found it worth their while to give freely of their steaks, too, since this bolstered their reputation.

Slocum mounted and walked his horse slowly until he came to a faint trail leading down to the flats where the herd was bedded down for the night. He squinted, hand shielding his eyes, as he slowly surveyed the area.

"Damn," he muttered.

"What's wrong? What'd you see, Slocum?" Garvin crowded close and tried to find what Slocum already had.

Slocum had worried that Pendergast had other plans than robbing the bank. The man was crookeder than a dog's hind leg, but why'd he have to rustle cattle right now?

"Come on," Slocum said, heading down the path. "We got ourselves some rustlers to catch."

12

"We gonna shoot it out with 'em?" Tom Garvin's eager voice worried Slocum. The six-shooter resting on the youngster's hip was proving too much of a novelty not to use. For all the skill he had shown cleaning the gun, he might end up killing half of Magnuson's trail hands if he opened up with it.

"If we have to. They're not taking a single head of this herd while I'm in charge." Slocum rolled the words around and tasted them, listened to the way they sounded, tried to weigh them against what he knew. It finally came to a simple idea. The others thought he was trail boss, so he was, no matter what Magnuson had said—or hadn't.

"Let's git 'em, then!"

"Whoa, hold on," Slocum said. Garvin was going for his six-gun. "We can't gallop a couple miles and get there in time or shape to do anything useful. We trot, we get to our outriders, *then* we get down to taking back our cattle."

Garvin pouted but thrust his six-shooter back into its holster. They made good time the couple miles to the back of the herd. The anxious cattle stirred as they approached.

The beeves still remembered the stampede. By morning this day's disaster would be forgotten.

"Get Jonesy," Slocum said to a rider who trotted up to see what he wanted. "I spotted rustlers."

"How many?"

"Saw four." Slocum didn't venture his opinion that he knew them. This had to be Pendergast. He had at least two more and maybe a half-dozen others in the gang. That was too much firepower to tackle all at once.

The cowboy cantered away, leaving Slocum and Garvin behind at the post he had abandoned.

"We kin git 'em ourselves. There's no need to get Jonesy or the others."

"You in a hurry to get yourself killed? I'd've thought this afternoon would have given you a close enough shave to last a week."

"Them's only cows," Garvin said dismissively. "These are outlaws!"

"One can kill you as dead as the other. Now hush up and listen." Slocum waited for Jonesy and the first cowboy to come over.

"I brung some spare ammo," Jonesy said. "You boys need it?"

Garvin still rode bareback. Whatever ammunition he needed had to be run through his S&W. Slocum saw the rest of them wore Colts, but his Colt Navy had been refitted to load .38 cartridges. The others carried .44s.

As Jonesy split his ammo with the other cowboy, Slocum sketched out what he had seen and what they had to do.

"Jonesy and I'll go after the rustlers. You and Garvin stay with the herd. Don't let any other rustler ride off with even so much as a flea off the back of any of our cattle."

"Slocum, I wanna go!"

"You don't even have a saddle. You need stirrups to stand up in to fight." Slocum shot Jonesy and the other cowboy a dark look as they snickered. Both knew why Slocum wanted

Garvin left behind. Hell, even Garvin knew. He was no one's fool.

"You see how many head they made off with already?"

"They might have as many as a dozen."

"Four men might not want to work with more 'n that," Jonesy said. Slocum didn't bother telling him that he knew the size of Pendergast's gang and that they could herd five times that.

"We'll have our hands full, no matter how many there are. You up to tangle with so many?"

Jonesy laughed. "I was born ready." He looked over his shoulder at the antsy Tom Garvin. "Him, now, he's learnin' to be ready. You meant the rustlers when you said there'd be a handful of trouble?"

"Garvin, too," Slocum said, having to smile.

"Can't say he's learned much, but what he's learned right's all been from you. That's why me and the boys'll follow you, Slocum. No two ways about it, we'd rather have Blassingame headin' up this drive, but you're doin' a good job."

"We're going to find out real quick," Slocum said. He pulled his Winchester from the sheath and saw how the wood stock had been cut up by flying hooves during the stampede. Unsure if the rifle still worked, he carefully levered a round into the chamber.

"How you want to handle this?"

"Just ride up and ask real polite for our cows back," Slocum said. He urged his mount forward, topped the small hillock, and saw four rustlers with a half-dozen head of Bar M cattle.

Never slowing, never rushing, Slocum rode straight for the outlaws. He didn't recognize any of them, but Pendergast might have more than had ridden behind him earlier.

"Who—" That was as far as one rustler got. Jonesy plugged him.

The other three went for their six-shooters. Slocum

dropped one and then the other two gave up, hands flying into the air. One pissed himself in his fright.

"Don't shoot. We give up!"

"Jonesy, no." Slocum saw that the cowboy was going to cut them down in cold blood. Under other circumstances, this was the best cattle thieves could hope for. Otherwise, they'd get their necks stretched when the nearest tree was found.

"Spoilsport," the cowboy grumbled. "Whatcha gonna do with 'em? No way we're guardin' 'em all the way to the rail-head."

"Pendergast," Slocum said loudly, watching the two men's reaction. Confusion. They exchanged looks, then stared up at Slocum.

"Mister, neither of us is anybody named Pendergast. Should we know 'em?"

"Probably help your cause if you did."

Slocum saw the lie forming on one man's lips—the one who had pissed all over himself. He caught himself and only looked frightened. The other shook his head.

"We ain't Pendergast, and we don't know anyone named that."

"What's that all about, Slocum?"

"Take two of the horses and gear—the dead men's," Slocum said to Jonesy. "And we drive back the beeves you've stolen." He glared at the two rustlers. It hardly seemed possible but the one who had pissed himself before did it again.

"What're you gonna do about us?"

"I'll cut you down where you stand if I ever set on eyes on either of you again," Slocum said in a tone that convinced both men they heard the gospel truth.

"You cain't jist let 'em go, Slocum!"

"Yes, I can," he declared.

The two surviving rustlers jumped into the saddle and rode like their tails were on fire.

"Shoulda kilt them. They'll only steal somebody else's cows."

"That's somebody else's worry." Slocum circled the bawling cattle and got them moving. Jonesy helped and they returned the steers to the herd a bit after sundown.

All the way back he kept thinking how this must have been some kind of test—or trap—laid down by Pendergast. Slocum knew rustlers would flock to a trail drive like flies to fresh cow flop. Picking up a stray or two was easy enough, and if the outriders weren't attentive enough, a hundred cattle might be cut from the herd. With enough unscrupulous ranchers willing to buy the cattle and mix them in with their own herd at the railhead, considerable money could change hands. And some of it would go to the purchasing agents, willing to overlook the different brands in a herd.

But the rustlers he had caught showed no sign of having heard of Pendergast. Slocum was a good enough poker player to read when a man was lying about his hand. The one surviving rustler would have said anything to get away alive—even lying about knowing Pendergast, if that had been his ticket to freedom. His partner had ridden a different road and denied knowing Pendergast, and Slocum reluctantly believed him.

They got back to the main herd. Slocum was bone-tired but made one last circuit to see that everything was going well. When he returned to their camp, he looked around.

"Somethin' chewin' on you, Slocum?" Jonesy asked.

"Where's Garvin?"

"Ain't seen him. Lemme ask around. Damn fool's as likely to git himself in more trouble than pluggin' himself in the chest with his own gun out here."

Slocum ate a can of beans and followed it with some peaches. The tinny taste burned his tongue, more because he worried about Garvin than the actual condition of the food in the airtights. He looked up when Jonesy returned.

"You ain't gonna believe this, Slocum. He lit out after the two cow thieves you let go."

"You mean he's out there taking the law into his own hands?"

Jonesy nodded, then squatted and started his own cold meal.

"Son of a bitch." Slocum got to his feet and went to saddle his horse.

"You ain't goin' after him, are you? Let him go, Slocum. He's not worth the trouble."

Slocum had vouched for the greenhorn, had shown him how to do the simpler tasks around a ranch, and now Garvin thought he knew it all. If he got the drop on the two outlaws, he might gun them down. There had been a wildness in his eye whenever he touched his six-shooter that bothered Slocum. He had seen enough killers in his day to recognize the bloodthirstiness building in the youngster.

"You keep everything calm, Jonesy," Slocum said, wheeling his horse around and heading into the twilight.

"If you don't let him be, you're as much a fool as he is," Jonesy shouted after him. Slocum couldn't argue with that. He felt like a complete dunderhead, but he was responsible for Garvin, just as he was for the rest of the trail crew.

He got his bearings from the early evening stars and traced his path back to where he and Jonesy had stopped the rustlers. The track to the spot where the two bodies still lay was easy to find in the dim light. The cattle he and Jonesy had recovered had left a trail a blind man could have followed.

He snorted in disgust. The two fleeing outlaws hadn't bothered to bury their partners. Dismounting, Slocum prowled about and saw that the bodies had been stripped of anything valuable. Their guns were missing, and torn pockets showed where hurried searches had found a watch or silver dollar tucked away.

Such behavior disgusted him. Jonesy had been right. If they hadn't hanged the two rustlers, they should have gunned them down on the spot.

A second circuit of the area showed the direction taken by the fleeing outlaws. Slocum lit a lucifer and studied the ground more closely.

Three horses.

Two rustlers and Tom Garvin.

He looked into the distance, and before the match burned his fingers, he thought he caught faint signs of their hoof-prints. He tossed the match aside, mounted, and started riding straight in the direction taken by the trio. For more than an hour he rode before he heard gunfire. Standing in the stirrups, he tried to get a better view ahead. The stars were his only illumination—and this let him find where the gun-shots came from.

Long tongues of yellow-orange leaped out from his left. To his right came a different report, sharper, with a blue-yellow flash. He sized up the situation quickly. Garvin was to the right, shooting with his Smith & Wesson. The two rustlers had pinned him down with rifle fire. The young cowboy didn't stand a chance because Slocum remembered Jonesy passing around boxes of ammunition. None of it had fit Garvin's pistol.

Whatever ammo he had was in his pistol and the loops in his gun belt. The way he returned fire, he would be out of luck soon.

Slocum put his heels to his horse and got it moving forward, heading for a halfway point. The rustlers wouldn't stay put when Garvin came up empty. They'd want to take out whoever had tried to kill them.

Deep in his gut Slocum knew that was the way it had gone down. Tom Garvin had opened fire on the two men, probably without announcing himself or giving them the chance to surrender. He might be wrong on this, but he doubted it. Worse, it hardly mattered. Garvin was in no position to run, and his ability to fight was dwindling rapidly.

Riding faster, Slocum heard the S&W come up empty. Muffled sounds followed. Garvin cursed as he either tried to reload or found he didn't have any more ammunition.

The two outlaws advanced quickly. For all their fear when he and Jonesy had caught them, the two worked well together now. One fired while the other advanced. When it became obvious to them Garvin wasn't returning their fire, either because he was wounded or had run out of cartridges, both advanced. Slocum reached a point where they crossed his line of sight. Both were too intent on their quarry to notice him level his Winchester and squeeze off a round.

One yelped. Slocum didn't have the certain feeling he had even winged him. That might have been a cry of surprise rather than pain. He fired with grim regularity until his magazine came up empty.

"Go get 'em, Garvin!" His order was intended to rout the rustlers. Not even Garvin would be foolish enough to actually rush the outlaws.

Slocum was wrong. Tom Garvin let out a shrill screech and ran forward, waving his pistol in the air. The moon had poked up enough above the horizon so that its light caught the S&W, turning it into a silvery sword waving above the man's head.

Against all logic, the frontal assault caused the outlaws to turn tail and run. If Garvin had any rounds left, he could have finished them. Slocum drew his Colt and fired carefully, but the range was too extreme for accurate shooting, even under the best of circumstances.

The pair ran uphill and disappeared. Slocum galloped forward and overtook Garvin. The cowboy ran as hard as he could. His breath came like a locomotive, and beads of sweat had turned to liquid silver on his forehead. For a moment Slocum hardly recognized him. It might have been the skull of a dead man rather than Garvin's face he saw.

"Slow down, dammit. Stop!" When Garvin showed no sign of obeying, Slocum drew even and kicked out, catching him between the shoulder blades and propelling him forward. Unable to keep his balance, Garvin skidded along in the dirt facedown.

He squirmed around, sat up, and waved his six-gun at Slocum.

"You—you can't do that! I almost had 'em!"

"Quiet," Slocum said. "You're out of ammo."

"They was runnin' fer their lives!"

Slocum held up his Colt Navy and said nothing. Garvin sucked in deep drafts of air and calmed down somewhat. He finally got to his feet and shoved his six-gun into his holster.

"I coulda caught them, Slocum. You stopped me from catchin' 'em!"

"How'd you have caught them, Tom?" He tried to sound calm, but his anger was almost at the boiling point.

"With this! I'd have hog-tied 'em!" Garvin held up his black rope. In the moonlight the silver strands glowed as if they were lit from within. "I'd've roped 'em!"

For a hoot and a holler Slocum would have let him try.

"You stay back of me. I've got the gun."

"Let me have your rifle. You can't shoot both at the same time."

"It's empty."

This finally hit Garvin with the seriousness of their position. If all Slocum had left were the rounds in his six-shooter, any attack was likely to end in their deaths. Garvin panted harshly and finally got his breath back.

"We're going to let them go. Let them think they got a posse on their asses."

"No!"

Before Slocum could knock some sense into the young

fool, the matter was determined for him. The two outlaws had decided to fight rather than run. Bullets whined past Slocum. He dived from the saddle, not wanting to lose another horse. Hitting the ground hard, he rolled and felt a sharp pain as a rock poked into his right elbow. It took a few seconds to shake the feeling back into the paralyzed arm.

When he looked around, he saw where one cattle thief had taken refuge. Garvin and the other were nowhere to be seen. Staying low, Slocum wormed his way uphill until he found a gully where he could take cover. And scant cover it provided, barely being deep enough for him to lie in so his back was level with the ground.

Two quick shots came, giving him both range and a spot to aim. The instant a third flash leaped out into the dark, he fired. Once, twice, a third time. He waited, but there wasn't any sound, no additional rifle fire. Nothing. He poked his hat up to draw fire. When a round didn't come to put a new hole in it, he scooted along the gully, got to his feet, and warily approached the tumble of rocks where the rustler sprawled on his back, raising sightless eyes to the beauty of the rising moon.

Slocum nudged him with his toe and got no response. He picked up the man's rifle and held it in the crook of his left arm as he searched the pockets for any hint that the rustler had lied earlier about knowing Pendergast. All he found was a sweaty wad of greenbacks totaling four dollars.

Having eliminated one threat, Slocum went up the hill, senses straining to find out what had happened to Garvin. He expected to find him with a bullet in his chest—smack through where his heart actually resided.

Choking sounds drew him to his left. Just on the other side of the small rise stood a tree. The moonlight glinted off the silver in Garvin's rope as it snaked over a limb and out of sight.

"You all right?" Slocum brought the rifle around when the gurgling sound suddenly stopped.

The rope slid back as the silhouette of a limp body swung into view.

"I roped 'im jist like I said I would, Slocum. Got the bastard!"

Garvin had dropped the loop over the man's neck, then used the tree limb to hoist him. Rather than having his neck broken cleanly by a knotted noose, the outlaw had strangled to death.

"Let him down."

"Why? He's for certain dead." Garvin released the rope. It made a slithering sound as it snaked over the limb and coiled itself atop the rustler's body.

Slocum dropped to one knee and pressed his fingers against the man's chest.

"Don't worry on that score, Slocum. He's dead." The boast in Garvin's voice almost made Slocum lash out at him. But he held his tongue. They had been in a fight for their lives. There wasn't call to braid down the cowboy for surviving. If anything, he had fought against a man who ought to have killed him easily.

He went through the dead man's pockets but found nothing but a nickel and a dime. He rocked back and sat heavily on the ground, watching the moonlight illuminate more of the corpse's features. As he had thought before, this wasn't one of Pendergast's men and nothing in his pockets had shown him to ride with the outlaw. But what would he have found to prove that? Outlaws weren't like lawmen. None of the rustlers riding with Pendergast wore badges proclaiming who they were.

Slocum felt suddenly tired, both physically and mentally. The outlaw had him by the balls so he saw the evil hand in everything that occurred.

"You want to split what I found?"

"What's that?"

"I got everything worth takin' from the other two, the ones you and Jonesy shot."

"You took time to rob them?"

"Ain't robbin' when they don't need it no more. All they had 'tween 'em was a pocket watch and eighteen cents." Garvin held it out in the palm of his hand.

"Keep it. You earned it," Slocum said bitterly.

"Don't need your permission to do that. And I want what was in this one's pockets. I kilt him fair and square, so it's all mine by right."

Slocum stood and tossed the two coins at Garvin's feet.

"Your blood money," he said. Without saying anything more, he started back to find his horse. He wanted this trail drive to be over as quick as possible so he wouldn't have to ride with Tom Garvin another mile.

13

"Another day, maybe two," Slocum said to Jonesy.

"You sound like you're glad it'll be over." The cowboy laughed. "Don't we all! I wanna get paid and laid, yes, sir, and a bottle. I want a bottle of popskull and am gonna get knee-walkin' drunk."

"It's good to know where you're headed," Slocum agreed.

"What you gonna tell the boss 'bout him?" Jonesy looked at Tom Garvin, who rode some distance away.

"What's to say? He's done his work so he ought to get paid like everyone else."

"You ain't sayin' a thing about that stampede or the rustlers?"

Slocum knew the cowboy doubted the wisdom of this, but he had decided. Garvin had settled down over the past week and had pulled his weight. More than once, his quick lariat had saved them all a passel of trouble. Roping a steer and wrestling it to the ground when it started to lead another stampede was as close to suicidal as Slocum had ever seen, but Garvin had pulled it off. He and his lariat had been just what they needed to make the rest of the trip to the rail yard safe and sound.

"Cain't believe he wrestled a steer like that. Hell and damnation, I bulldogged for a spell and threw my back out of place with a calf a quarter the size. He's one lucky son of a bitch."

"Seems to go in spells," Slocum said. "Shooting himself was pure bad luck. And there's been about as much bad to go with the good."

"Still alive, still in the saddle, that makes him a winner, I reckon," Jonesy said. "I'd just as soon ride a different trail." He paused, then added, "But with you, Slocum, I'll sign on any time. You know the country, you know the herd. It's 'cuz of you we got through this quick."

"Not so sure we're through yet," Slocum said, eyeing the sky. Heavy black clouds blew in from the northwest, the usual storm track this time of year. The clouds even crackled with lightning.

"Rain's no problem, 'less we get flash flooding."

"Might do just that," Slocum said. He studied the terrain ahead and worried about how flat it was. The deep ravines had been cut by rapidly flowing water—like that promised by the storm moving their way fast enough that he saw the clouds sailing along. As he watched, the sun vanished behind a cloud heavy with rain.

"We kin outrun it," Jonesy said.

Slocum doubted that was possible. A tiny raindrop already splatted against the brim of his hat, rolled about, and then dripped wetly onto his saddle. The smell preceding a heavy rain filled the air with a curious sharp scent. A sudden bolt of lighting too near for comfort caused his horse to rear. Slocum got it under control, then looked around for higher ground.

"We need to bed down for the storm. No way we can keep the herd moving. This is going to be a real frog strangler."

"If you say so," Jonesy said skeptically. "Wrong time of

year for big rain. This'll blow over in an hour. Been dry so far, so why's it gonna catch up now?"

"Higher ground that way," Slocum said, finding the part of the countryside that afforded the only sanctuary in a really heavy downpour. "Let's start moving the beeves."

Jonesy rode off, grumbling to himself. Slocum went the other direction and convinced the cowboys to do more than get out their yellow slickers.

"Is it gonna be bad, Slocum?" Tom Garvin looked a tad frightened. "I don't like storms. They always scared me when I was a kid."

Slocum refrained from asking how many weeks ago that was. If anything, he wanted Garvin to shut up rather than ramble on.

"Got so bad I hid under my bed sometimes. Me and my dog. Ole Ben ran out into the rain and got struck by lightning." Garvin shuddered. "Still remember the smell."

"There'll be cooking beef if we don't get the herd settled down."

"That's kinda hard with all this noise." Garvin's words were almost drowned out by a heavy clap of thunder. The storm moved closer fast.

In less than ten minutes the rain fell so hard and heavy Slocum could barely see a dozen yards in front of him. He hoped Jonesy and the rest of the crew were doing their part to keep the herd moving because the ground turned spongy and then muddy. Not far to his left a bank of an existing ravine fell in as water rushed down it. There might not be an inch of rainfall in an hour, but when the entire prairie funneled the downpour into a few rivers, riding became dangerous.

Slocum used his rope to swat the rump of a steer to keep it moving where he thought uphill might be. The rain hit the ground so hard now droplets danced back a good six inches. When the dirt turned entirely to mud, the land began flowing. Using that downward direction as a guide, Slocum kept the cattle moving opposite.

It was hard to tell if he had reached the dubious summit of the small hill. Riding around the edge of the herd helped keep the cattle bunched together. They naturally sought one another for protection against the driving rain, making his job a little easier. Some went down to the ground while others crowded above them. By the time he had completed a circuit, he found Jonesy.

"Slocum, if ever I doubt you ag'in, you kin jist whomp me in the head to knock some sense back in. This is turnin' into a real storm."

"We need to keep the herd bedded down. I don't think they'll try to run because of the thunder, but they're dumb as dirt."

"It's gonna be a long night if the storm hangs on like it's lookin' to," Jonesy said. He scowled and asked, "How long 'til sundown anyway? It's darker than a coal miner's soul right now, and it cain't be past two."

"That's about right," Slocum said, not taking his watch out to check. It didn't matter what the time was. All that counted was riding out the storm.

"You see Garvin?"

"No," Slocum said. "Can't say I was looking for him, though."

"If anybody's gonna git into trouble, my money's on him. I didn't see hide nor hair of him. Did everybody else? Want me to find him?"

"You go one way around the herd, I'll go the other. We can meet up on the far side."

Slocum took better than twenty minutes to see Jonesy riding stolidly through the rain. From the set to the cowboy's shoulders, he knew he hadn't found Tom Garvin either.

"Where do you suppose he got off to?" Jonesy asked.

Slocum backtracked mentally on how they had formed the herd and gotten it moving to the rapidly eroding knoll. In spite of the mudflows, this was the safest spot he had found for the herd to stay. Lower areas would erode even faster as rain ran downhill into the flooded gullies.

"He might have gotten on the wrong path a half mile back," Slocum said. "The ravine was shallow, but the water flowed fast."

"Cain't wade through even a shallow one," Jonesy said. "I got my feet knocked from under me with only an inch of flowin' water on my first drive. The others in the crew laughed themselves sick. Never let me fergit."

"He might be stranded on the far side of the ravine by now," Slocum said.

"Then he ain't in no danger."

They looked at each other through a wet curtain. Jonesy snorted in disgust.

"Want me to hunt fer him?"

"I'll go. I feel responsible," Slocum said.

"You might have to wait 'til the rain's over to even find us again. A man kin git lost mighty quick in a torrential rain like this."

"If I'm not back when the storm lets up, keep moving toward town. We can't be more than ten or fifteen miles away."

"A day, maybe two."

"A day," Slocum said positively.

"You don't show up, I ain't holdin' back on my drinkin' and whorin'."

"Start the celebration without me. But I'll be there. *We'll* be there."

Jonesy spat and waved Slocum off as if he was shooing away a buzzing fly. Turning his reluctant horse downhill, he slipped and slid in the rivulets of mud and came to a level patch. Slocum could only guess direction since the trail was nothing but sticky mud now. Any track of a hoofprint had long since been erased.

He pulled his hat down a little more to shield his eyes and pressed on in the rain. Not being able to see more than a few yards made him wonder if this was a fool's errand. Garvin would be fine if he simply found a high spot and settled down until the storm passed. That was the sensible thing.

That gnawed at Slocum. It was the *sensible* thing. He wasn't sure he had seen much that was sensible out of the tenderfoot. If anything, Garvin grew increasingly irresponsible as he thought his experience made him into a seasoned cowboy.

Slocum yanked back on the reins, bringing his horse to a sudden halt. The horse tried to toss its head in protest of the bit cutting so hard into his mouth, but Slocum didn't want to move an inch farther. The ravine he had seen—one hardly three feet across—now spanned more than five feet and was filled with roiling, muddy water. The current was so fast no man could ride across without being swept away.

He peered through the rain and murk and saw a flash of silver against black. Garvin's damned rope.

"Can you get across the water?" Slocum shouted. Garvin jerked about and looked up.

"The ground's meltin' out from under me!"

"The rain's coming down even harder. You aren't safe there."

The small island of dirt was eroding visibly as the storm-fed river rose and boiled about. Garvin would be sucked into the maelstrom in a few minutes unless he did something.

"I can't go anywhere, Slocum. I was cut off."

Slocum wondered what the hell Garvin had been up to, but this was no time to ask such questions. For two cents he would leave him to his fate, but he felt responsible. Garvin was his own man, and increasingly so, but Slocum had taken him under his wing. Letting him die wasn't going to happen. He would do all he could to save any of the other trail hands, even if they weren't likely to wander off in a fierce storm.

If Garvin tried riding his horse across the increasingly deep river, he and the horse would be swept away. Slocum took a deep breath. The young cowboy's only chance was to abandon his gear and try to cross the raging river without his horse.

"Can you throw me the end of your rope? You need to use it to cross the water."

"Leave my horse? I can't do that!"

"You're going to die if you don't." Slocum took his own rope, played out a small loop, then began spinning it over his head. He let it fly. The storm wind caught the rope and lifted it.

Then it fell feet short of reaching Garvin.

Slocum stepped closer and cast the rope again. Again the rope flew straight and true—and inches short. Before he could step even closer to make up the last few inches, the bank began turning to sludge under his boots, forcing him to step away. There was no hope at all of throwing the rope to Garvin to rescue him.

"My rope's too short," Slocum called. He wiped water from his face. The sheets of blowing rain parted for a moment, giving him a good view of Garvin. The island where he stood had been cut down to a space hardly three feet across.

"My rope's longer," Garvin said. "Isn't there a way to save my horse? I can ride it—"

The anguished screech of the horse blotted out his words. The ground had been cut from under the horse's hooves, catapulting it into a turbulent stream. Its head bobbed above the murky brown surface, then it vanished. All cries were drowned out by the sound of the water—and by drowning.

"Throw your rope," Slocum shouted. He had no faith that the black rope would be long enough, but it was Garvin's only hope.

Tom Garvin spun the rope over his head and then loosed it. As Slocum's had, it lofted, was caught by the wind, and brought across the river. It fell feet short, too.

Before Slocum could sign Garvin's death warrant by

telling him to try swimming across, the cowboy pulled back the rope and coiled it for another try. This time it seemed to stretch, to grow longer. The silver threads chasing the length blazed as lightning lashed the sky. And the rope fell at Slocum's feet.

He stamped down hard and pressed the end of the rope into the ground to keep it from being pulled back toward the river by the gusty wind. Slocum dropped to his knee and grabbed the rope. It felt hot in his hands. He sat, dug in his feet, and knew he could never give a strong enough anchor for Garvin to get across.

Slocum looked around for something to fasten the end of the rope. A jagged rock had been washed up out of the ground.

"Let me fasten the rope. I can't hold it by myself." He stretched the rope as taut as he could, got it looped around the rock. He kicked a couple times to be sure the rock was securely embedded.

Slocum cinched the rope down, braced his feet so he could tug and pull Garvin across.

"Jump!"

Slocum wiped rain from his eyes and saw that Garvin had no choice. The river had completely eaten away his small island of safety. The cowboy splashed into the river. The sudden jerk on the rope unbalanced Slocum. He braced his foot against the rock and began pulling on the rope. The loop was like a poor pulley, but Slocum put his back to the effort.

Inch by inch he pulled Garvin closer to the safety of the riverbank.

"I'm almost there, Slocum. Almost there!"

Slocum pulled harder and then slammed flat on his back as the rock came free of the ground. The rock landed atop him, and he lost his grip on the rope.

Tom Garvin was swept away in the flood-swollen river.

14

Slocum stared at his rope-burned hands and then through the downpour into the river. The way it churned prevented him from getting any idea where Tom Garvin might have gone. Being swept away in that millrace wasn't the worst way to die, Slocum supposed. Garvin would probably have his head smashed against a rock and drown pretty fast. There was no way anyone could possibly fight the current. With the ravine being cut ever deeper by the flash flood, no chance existed for Garvin to be washed onto a bank.

Slocum wiped water from his face, then backed from the river as another couple feet of once-solid ground collapsed and became part of the deadly current. The mud made it impossible to see down into the water. There was a small chance Garvin might have caught on a root sticking out into the river as the water eroded dirt around trees and bushes.

He backed off another foot when a larger section of the land simply sank, a small eddy pool forming in front of him. Despair filled him at the loss. He had liked Garvin at first, then had come to feel some rancor toward him as his arrogance grew. He was sorry to see a life snuffed out so fast, no matter how he'd ended up thinking of the young man.

Mounting, Slocum rode slowly along the riverbank, trying to get his bearings to return to the herd. Jonesy was a competent drover and would have everything under control, but Slocum felt the increasing need to be done with the drive.

Mostly he wanted to get the herd to market, then return to the Bar M and talk with Christine. Everything from the trail drive had convinced him even more that settling down was a good idea, but he needed to know where he stood with her. Mordecai Magnuson pushed her toward the neighboring rancher's son. That made economic sense. A spread twice the size of the Bar M had a better chance of surviving. Slocum had seen bad times and good. The Panic of '73 had driven too many ranchers into bankruptcy. The survivors were the larger ranches.

The Bar M with the Norton ranch would be the largest in the area and control prices for the beeves. It made financial sense for Christine to marry Josh Junior.

It made no sense at all to Slocum if she found the younger rancher as obnoxious as she claimed. The memory of her with Norton at the square dance still burned in his brain, though. They hadn't danced as if she found him all that disagreeable, though she might have been on her best behavior because both her pa and Norton were there watching. Better to pretend than to cause a scene. Away from the crowd it might be different.

It had to be different. Slocum's intentions toward her were nothing but honorable.

With a strong hand on the reins to replace Jed Blassingame, Slocum could double the profitability of the Bar M. That had to appeal to Magnuson if his only reason of marrying Christine off was to enhance his income.

The tree in his path caused Slocum to jerk back on the reins. His thoughts had been miles away, and the heavy rain was only now letting up a mite to allow him to see more than a few yards ahead. The wind and rain had stripped most of the leaves off the tree, but the way it bent showed it wasn't dead.

He stared at it, something bothering him. Why did it bend almost double—and against the wind? It should have bent with the wind.

Returning to the herd prodded him to ignore this small mystery, but curiosity had always been his bane. Slocum rode closer and saw that something had tangled in the upper limbs. From the vibration, whatever was caught surged and ebbed with the water running in the river.

"Son of a bitch," he muttered. A distant flash of lighting illuminated the tree—and the black rope with silver threads wrapped around the upper limbs. The taut rope stretched downward at an angle into the river.

Slocum dismounted and ran to the tree. Arms around the sturdy trunk, he peered over the embankment into the raging water. The swift stream had washed away dirt around half the tree's roots. They flopped about like weird wooden brown fingers, but in the middle of the tangle he saw the top of Tom Garvin's head.

The cowboy clung to his rope with a fierce tenacity that had undoubtedly saved his life. How he had roped the upper part of the tree while being swept along wasn't something Slocum could figure out. Better to ask Garvin straight out.

Slocum flopped onto his belly and reached out.

"Garvin! You alive? Grab hold. I'll pull you up."

A dirty, strained face lifted. Garvin blinked muddy water from his eyes and tried to speak. He choked on a mouthful of river. Spitting it out, he put his head down and pulled hard on the rope. Slocum caught the rope and tried to pull him up. The rope felt as if it were on fire.

He released it, thinking he had too badly burned his hands earlier for this to be a way to save Garvin. Slocum scooted perilously close to the embankment, feeling it yielding under his chest. Slocum hooked his toes around an exposed root and strained to reach down to the surface of the river. As Garvin bobbed up, Slocum caught his wrist and yanked with all his strength. Muscles in his belly protested the load and his knees sank into the soft earth.

But the cowboy shot upward out of the water and crashed down against the tangle of exposed roots. Garvin instinctively wrapped his arms around the wood until Slocum could give another solid pull. Rolling onto his back, Slocum almost threw Garvin onto more solid ground.

The cowboy clung to his black rope as if his life depended on it. Slocum looked upward and knew that Garvin's life *had* depended on that rope. Without it being looped around the upper tree limbs, he would have been swept away and drowned.

"You all right? Or as good as you can be after almost getting yourself drowned like a rat?"

Garvin sputtered and spat water, then retched. When the spasm passed, he used the rope to pull himself up to a sitting position under the tree. Blinking hard, he finally focused on Slocum.

"Didn't expect to see you ag'in, Slocum."

"That makes two of us. Come on, can you stand?" Slocum got his arms around the man's shoulders and pulled him to his feet.

Garvin sagged, and Slocum had to strain to support even his slight weight. It surprised him how weak he felt. Pulling Garvin from the river had taken more out of him than he'd thought possible.

"Walk. Get your feet moving."

"I'm doin' fine. Let me be."

Slocum backed off, watching closely, and decided Garvin was right. For a man battered by the water and smashed into the sides of the ravine for a couple miles, he was in good shape. Garvin tugged on the rope and used it to support himself until he could send a wave sailing upward. Slocum jumped back when the black rope came free with only this small twitch of Garvin's wrist.

"How did that hold you? It wasn't even looped around the tree, was it?"

"Saved me, Slocum. It damned well saved me." Garvin clutched the rope to his chest like a lover and cooed to it.

"We'll have to ride double," Slocum said, unnerved by Garvin's actions.

Garvin coiled his rope and, by the time Slocum had stepped up into the saddle, was ready to swing up behind. He held the rope in one hand and circled Slocum's waist with the other. Sagging, he almost fell off the horse but caught himself in time.

Slocum rode slowly, aware of how Garvin clung to consciousness by a thread. It took almost an hour of wending their way through the still considerable rain to find the herd. Riding into the small camp caused the cowboys there to gape in wonder.

"You looked like a drowned prairie dog," Jonesy said, staring up at Garvin.

"Help him down. He's still feeling a bit rocky." As if to prove Slocum's point, Garvin fell off the horse. Jonesy caught him, staggered back, then lowered him to the ground.

"Don't reckon gettin' muddier is a concern. Swear he must have river water in his veins by now." Jonesy looked hard at Slocum. "You pulled him out of the river?"

"Get him by the fire." Slocum looked around. The rain made it impossible to light a fire. "Put a blanket over him, then cover that with a slicker. Catching pneumonia and dying would be a crying shame after what he's been through."

Jonesy tried to pry the rope from Garvin's grip and got a feral snarl as a warning.

"He's strong enough to do that himself." Jonesy walked off to huddle with the other cowboys. They cast occasional frightened glances in Garvin's direction.

Slocum set about doing what he'd asked Jonesy to do. Garvin wouldn't appreciate it, but it was the right thing to do. Once the cowboy was covered, Slocum stepped back and stared at him, wondering what dreams ran through the man's head. A curious smile and a look of triumph made Garvin look like he was the cat that had just eaten the canary.

"Rain's lettin' up, Slocum," Jonesy said. "You want to press on? We kin make a couple miles 'fore it gets too dark."

"The ground is slippery. Let the sun come out and dry it up a mite," Slocum said. "Tomorrow is good enough. Let the cattle rest up. They've got more travel ahead of them."

"Knowin' where they're goin', they ought to want to ride on the trail forever," Jonesy said, chuckling.

"That's why they don't know," Slocum said. He looked back at Garvin and wondered if the same was true with the sleeping cowboy. Did he know where he was going and should he just keep riding rather than arrive at the slaughterhouse?

"The weight's burnin' off the beeves," Jonesy said. "Mr. Magnuson ain't gonna like the condition they're in."

"He can leave them in a feed lot for a day or two if that's a concern," Slocum said. "He won't find these cows in any worse shape than those brought in from other ranches."

"I don't know. Norton started earlier. His herd might not have gone through the rain."

Slocum couldn't believe how difficult it had been moving the herd after the rain. The sun hadn't come out to dry the soggy ground, forcing the cattle to use extra energy to slog along. Grass had been harder to locate, and the beeves had turned balky. Rather than one day to get to the railhead, it had taken three. Still, in spite of the struggle or maybe because of it, Slocum didn't think he had ever seen a prettier sight than the stockyards and the nearby rail yard with two locomotives parked, long strings of empty cattle cars waiting for their freight.

"I'll go tell Magnuson we've arrived."

"Reckon he'll be at the broker's office," Jonesy said. "That's the building off to the side, away from the pens."

"You want to come along?"

"Naw, I prefer the company of the steers. Listenin' to them ranchers lyin' through their store-bought teeth gives me the collywobbles. Just git us our money and all will be jist fine."

Garvin spoke up. "I'll go with you. I want to hear how they dicker."

"Still thinkin' on bein' foreman?" Jonesy asked.

"I will be. You wait and see."

Jonesy laughed and the mirth rippled through the other trail hands. Garvin bristled. When he rested his hand on the S&W at his hip, Slocum said, "Come on along, Garvin. They can handle the cattle for a while without us."

"Sons of bitches. I'll show 'em, I'll show the whole damned lot of them!"

"We've been on the trail for ten days," Slocum said, "and everyone's tuckered out. Losing Hashknife and the chuck wagon wore on everybody, too."

"They're a bunch of—"

"Come on," Slocum said sharply. He regretted asking Garvin to accompany him, but letting him stay with the others would create friction that too easily might erupt into gunplay. Jonesy wouldn't take any guff off Garvin, and Garvin was itching to get into a gunfight.

Tom Garvin took the loop of his rope and slid it over his head, wearing it like a Mexican *bandido* with his bandolier. With it over his right shoulder and dangling at his left hip, he kept his S&W handy on his right side.

Slocum rode slowly through town, feeling the expectation all around. There was a nervous tension among the townspeople that was communicated to him. They were anxious for the cowboys to spend their money. They made huge profits off brokering the sale of the herds and the shipment back East, and the citizens were all counting on earning enough to live an entire year until the next trail drive.

"They're all starin' at me. They think I'm a nuthin'," Garvin said.

"You aren't anything," Slocum said. He hurried on when Garvin bristled. "Jingle some silver dollars together and you'll be their best friend in the world."

"I don't pay for my friends."

Slocum refused to rise to the bait. Garvin was spoiling for a fight, and he wouldn't give it to him. He settled down in the saddle and rode slowly, hunting for the building Jonesy had mentioned and getting the feel of the town. After the time on the trail, so many people crowded in on all sides. He both liked it and feared it. Open horizons and empty prairies were more to his liking than people all crowded together.

"There," he said. "You want to watch the horse."

"Think they'd steal 'em?" Garvin set his jaw and would gun down anyone getting too close.

"Not with you looking so fierce," Slocum said.

Garvin frowned, not sure how to take the words. Slocum didn't give him time to decide. He dismounted and went into the office. The large room was lined with desks, clerks poring over their ledgers. At the far side a better-dressed man who might have been a banker sat back smoking a cigar. Across the desk from him Mordecai Magnuson puffed furiously on a stogie of his own. The broker pointed at Slocum with the lit end of his cigar, said something to Magnuson, then puffed away so hard his face vanished in a cloud of blue smoke.

Slocum strode over, touched the brim of his hat, and said, "Herd's out by the pens, Mr. Magnuson."

"Took your sweet time getting here, didn't you, Slocum?"

"We had some trouble."

"Tell me later. How many head did you lose?"

"Not more than a hundred."

"That's good, but you ran all the fat off them, didn't you?"

"It was a harder trail than you said." Slocum worked to keep down his anger. Garvin had irked him, but Magnuson went out of his way to needle him.

"Blassingame should have been foreman."

Slocum was in no mood to argue the point. Losing the cook and so much equipment, staying on the trail with only the food scavenged from the destroyed chuck wagon, the rain, and the rest had worn his temper thin.

"You ready to pay us?"

"You're jumping the gun, Slocum. I need to negotiate with Mr. Dunlap before that."

"How long'll it take?"

"You got yourself a pushy trail boss, Mordecai. I can't blame him, though. It's always good to be paid for your hard work." Dunlap craned to one side and peered around Slocum. "There's my appraiser. Let's see what he has to say."

Dunlap's man had waited for the herd to be put into pens, then he counted them and gave his estimate of the value. Slocum stepped back and let the rancher and the broker dicker. The size of the settlement made him wonder if a bonus might not be in the offing. He watched Dunlap count out stacks of greenbacks, then hand over a large leather sack filled with twenty-dollar gold pieces. This went into Magnuson's coat pocket. The paper money would be used to pay the trail hands.

"Thank you, Mr. Dunlap," Magnuson said, standing. "Always a pleasure doing business with a gentleman."

"Take a few more—to get you back home to your own supply," Dunlap said, pushing a box of cigars to the rancher.

"Come on, Slocum. We got some settling up to do." Magnuson strode out, not waiting to see if Slocum trailed along behind.

They stepped into the bright sunlight.

"You go on, Mr. Magnuson," Slocum said. "My cinch strap needs tightening. I'll catch up in a minute." Slocum put his hand against his horse's side to keep it in place. The broad leather cinch had been cut almost through somewhere on the trail. He could ride a little while longer, but before returning to the Bar M, he had to get the saddle to the town saddle maker for repair.

Magnuson grunted and mounted his horse. Garvin hastily joined him, riding alongside. What the two men might have to say baffled Slocum, but they were talking as if they were old friends. He shrugged it off and saw where one of the holes in the leather cinch had torn, making the saddle slip. Driving his knee into the horse's belly to be sure it had emptied its lungs, Slocum cinched the saddle down one more notch. It wouldn't be comfortable for the horse, but Slocum didn't expect to ride this way very long.

As soon as he got paid, he'd have it fixed properly.

Gunshots echoed from the direction taken by Magnuson and Garvin. For a moment, crazy things flashed through his mind. Garvin had shot Magnuson. Magnuson had shot Garvin. Slocum swung into the saddle and galloped after them.

He found them in a side street. Two men moaned and writhed about on the ground.

"Road agents, Slocum, these road agents tried to rob Mr. Magnuson but I stopped 'em!" A smoking six-gun in Garvin's hand gave mute testimony to that.

"Why were you not riding along with us, Slocum? Never mind. Garvin saved me from being robbed—and saved your pay. You and the rest of the crew ought to thank him."

By now the marshal and two deputies had come running up, waving sawed-off shotguns around. They were getting ready for a bunch of rowdy cowboys in their town and were loaded for bear.

Slocum watched the lawman get the two robbers to their feet and move them along to the town lockup. He had made a point of getting a good look at the robbers' faces. Neither was a member of Pendergast's gang.

He almost dared to hope that Pendergast had moved on. But Slocum knew that wasn't likely with so much money from the cattle sale to be stolen. When the other ranchers put their year's income into the town bank, Pendergast would strike then.

Slocum started to warn Magnuson, but the rancher cut him off with a brusque wave of his hand. Trailing the rancher and Garvin made him feel like a servant, but he did work for Magnuson.

And there was the matter of his boss's daughter. Slocum couldn't forget Christine, no matter how poorly her pa treated him.

15

"Quite a drive, wasn't it, Slocum?" Tom Garvin crowed like the cock of the walk. "Yes, sir, and it ended up real good, 'specially for me."

"Good of Magnuson to give you a reward for saving his hide from those thieves."

"I'd had a real run of bad luck 'fore that. Better for me to be in the right place than you." Garvin rode closer. "You didn't have nuthin' to do with that robbery, did you?"

Slocum looked at him sharply. All the way back from the railhead Garvin had skirted around asking this very question. Now that they rode under the arch with Bar M brand emblazoned on it, he finally felt confident enough to ask.

"No."

"You coulda made a passel of money."

"So could you," Slocum said. "You wouldn't even have needed to rob a dead man."

"Ah, them bastards didn't need what they had in their pockets." Garvin pulled out a watch and held it up, letting it swing slowly in the bright sunlight. Somehow, the golden gleam wasn't what it should have been, but that might have been Slocum remembering how he had taken it from a man he had gunned down with no good reason.

The four rustlers were an annoyance and nothing more for Slocum. Two had died trying to shoot it out. That was their bad luck. But Garvin had gone after the other two when they wouldn't have caused any more trouble—had gone after them with the sole purpose of shooting them down.

"How you going to spend your reward? You have a lot more than the rest of us." Slocum tasted some bitterness with those words. Magnuson hadn't paid him top hand wages. Slocum might as well have ridden along on the drive and nothing more without the stress of being the trail boss. Without him, they would have lost a hundred or more head than had reached the feed pens alive and kicking.

"Not sure yet. Maybe get myself a better saddle. This one's fallin' apart from the trail."

Slocum looked at his own saddle and had to agree this was a decent investment to make. Taking care of his gear in the middle of stampedes and gully washers hadn't been all that easy.

"Thinkin' on gettin' me a rifle, too. And a lot of ammo for my trusty iron." Garvin slapped his right side. The S&W hardly moved at the newfound attention.

"Just don't use one of the rounds to shoot yourself," Slocum said, riding ahead to the bunkhouse and leaving Garvin to grumble about smart-ass remarks.

Slocum dismounted and went inside. He considered sprawling out on the bunk and grabbing some shut-eye, but something else worried at him. After stowing his saddlebags under his bunk, he led his horse to the barn, took care of his gear and the horse the best he could, then went looking for the reason he had bothered returning to the Bar M.

Christine Magnuson had to be around somewhere.

He poked his head into the kitchen. The oven was cool and there weren't any signs Christine had even thought of starting supper for her pa. That meant she was out on the range somewhere, maybe gathering herbs for her cooking. Slocum knew the exact spot where she'd go.

Trooping down an arroyo, he cut up the steep bank after a quarter mile and went into a stand of oak trees. Strands of poison oak crept around some of the trees, and he avoided those the best he could, though he got tangled in a briar bush before he found the game trail through the woods that Christine always followed. He had approached it from the side. If he followed it to his left, it led back to the ranch house.

He went to the right and heard a musical sound from ahead. Christine was singing to herself as she plucked the various plants, roots, and leaves for her cooking.

"You sing mighty purty," Slocum said.

Christine jumped, saw who he was, and put her hand to her throat. She let out a huge sigh. The sight of her breasts rising and falling under her bodice distracted Slocum from what he had intended to say.

"You snuck up on me, John. You know better 'n to do that. I might have shot you."

"You carrying a gun?"

"No, but I might have been." She moved her half-full basket of greens around and sat on a stump. With great deliberation, she lifted one leg up and put her foot on the stump so her skirt hiked up, giving Slocum a tantalizing view of bare leg.

"Reckon I'd have to come to your rescue if you got into trouble."

"What kind of trouble do you anticipate me getting into?" she asked impishly. With a slow movement, she rocked her knee to one side, giving him a view of her bare inner thigh—and higher.

"Looks like somebody stole your undies."

"Do tell? Well, my observant marshal, maybe you'd better check the scene of the crime for clues." Christine rocked back on the stump, both hands behind her so she could get her other foot onto the stump while keeping her knees spread wide.

Slocum had other business with her, but that could wait. He put his hands on her knees and held them apart when she tried to close up.

"Why, I do declare. Are you going to take advantage of me?" She batted her eyelashes at him. "Poor li'l ole me!"

He dropped to his knees and kissed first one snowy thigh and then the other. She moaned softly as he worked his way up to the thick bush between her legs. His tongue slid out and raked along her nether lips. The pinkly scalloped flaps began to tremble as he licked and sucked, kissed and tongued her most sensitive flesh.

"Oh, Detective Slocum, what are you finding there?"

"The scene of the crime. Something's missing."

"Whatever could that be?" She gasped when he ran his finger into her and began flexing it. She gasped and sobbed and leaned back farther. "I-It's not that. That's not supposed t-to be th-there."

"What else could it be?"

"You," she said in a sex husky voice. "I want you in there."

"Another finger?" He began stroking in and out, slathering her inner lubricants all around.

"No! Your dick! I want *you* in me! I need *it* in me!"

With her sitting on the stump, Slocum didn't see how that would be possible. He ran his hands around and caught up the doughty lumps of her ass cheeks. He squeezed down, causing her to moan even louder. As she rocked forward, he got his feet under him and lifted. Christine was light and sailed upward.

A quick spin and she had her legs wrapped around his waist, his crotch pressed into her naked one. Slocum sat down fast so they reversed positions.

"Your turn to play hide and seek."

"Seek," she said. "Yes, definitely I want to seek . . . this!"

She worked his fly buttons open and released the raging stallion behind those cloth gates. Her mouth engulfed the tip. She teased it with her tongue and lips, then shoved it out.

"Seek and hide!" She straddled his waist, one foot on either side of the stump. Then she lowered herself around his groin. The thick top of his manhood brushed past the nether lips he had already kissed and rested in the moist crease for a moment.

Neither of them could speak as sensations ripped through them, filled their minds and bodies with a passion not to be contained. She reached down, grabbed hold, and guided his shaft to her pink gates. Simply relaxing and letting gravity do its work, she took him full length up into her heated center.

Again they were robbed of speech. Then Christine gasped out, "So big. You're so big in me."

Slocum reached up and pressed his hand into her bodice, feeling the firm, lush breasts beneath. Hard buttons capped each of those marshmallowy mounds. Through her blouse he pressed down hard and elicited a gasp of even greater desire from her. Christine threw back her head and turned her face to the cloudless blue autumn sky.

She let out tiny sounds that grew as she rose and fell around his thick, fleshy pillar. When she began twisting on every descent, Slocum felt the pressures mounting in his loins that couldn't be contained much longer. He closed his eyes and let the hot sensation spread throughout his groin, his belly, his entire body. Reaching out, he cupped her buttocks and guided her in a rhythm that built even more sexual tension.

And then he could hold back no longer. Arching his back and trying vainly to thrust upward off the stump, he felt himself totally engulfed in hot, damp female flesh that grasped and squeezed and caressed his hidden length.

He exploded.

And seconds later, Christine went berserk, pumping fast

and hard until he began to turn limp within her. She gasped, and rocked back to look at him. Her face was covered with sex sweat, and she positively glowed.

"I don't know what to say, John."

"Again?"

She laughed and stood, straightening her skirts, letting them fall down to a more chaste level.

"In your dreams. You couldn't—" Christine spun at a bull-throated roar of rage.

"Papa!" She took a step forward, giving Slocum a moment to tuck himself back in and try to button his fly. He only got one fastened before Mordecai Magnuson charged out of the woods like a bull attacking a red flag.

"What the hell's going on?" He swung a shotgun around and pushed his daughter out of the way.

Slocum found himself staring down the double barrels of a ten-gauge that would blow him to bloody bits.

"I saw your daughter and came to see if she needed any help."

Magnuson glanced at his daughter and the flush on her cheeks.

"You been havin' your way with her, Slocum? I'll kill you here and now if you have!"

"Papa, please. It's not like that."

Slocum started to declare his love for the woman. He swung forward to get to his feet, but the shotgun barrel swung back, hard, fast, and caught him on the side of the head. He sprawled on the forest floor, stunned by the blow. Bees buzzed about and he couldn't focus his eyes.

In the far distance he heard, "If I could prove you molested her, I'd kill you outright."

"Papa, you—"

"Shut up. Get on back to the house."

Slocum grunted as a boot struck him hard in the ribs. He rose to hands and knees and caught another one in the belly that took the starch out of him. He collapsed to the ground.

"You're fired, Slocum. I knew there was something wrong with you. I should have fired you before the trail drive but I was shorthanded."

Slocum gasped as another kick to his midsection sent waves of pain through his body where pleasure had dwelled only a few minutes earlier. The Magnuson family took him from one physical extreme to the other.

"If I lay eyes on you, I'll shoot first. I swear, Slocum, I'll kill your sorry ass and not regret it for an instant."

Slocum braced for another kick, but it never came. He lay panting until he got his breath back. He rolled over and looked around. Both Magnuson and Christine had gone, but she had left her basket of herbs behind. Getting to his feet, Slocum doubled over in pain, staggered, and supported himself on the stump where he and Christine had made love.

"Son of a bitch," Slocum said. He kicked the basket of herbs and then followed the game trail, knowing it would lead back to the ranch house. He'd have it out with Magnuson once and for all.

Christine would choose him over her pa, and they could make a life for themselves as far away as possible.

Somehow, Slocum got lost. He might have taken a wrong branch in the trail or simply left the trail by accident and taken another. It was almost sundown when he got back to the bunkhouse.

He went in and sat heavily on his bed. He gently probed his ribs. There didn't seem to be anything broken, but the bruises were livid, ugly yellows and purples in the shape of Magnuson's toe.

"Wondered when you'd git back," came a cold voice.

He looked up to see Tom Garvin in the doorway, his hand resting on the butt of his six-shooter.

"Where's Magnuson? I want to have words with him."

"He and Miss Christine have left. Gone for a ride."

"Where? When'll they be back?"

"Cain't rightly say, and it don't matter because you're gettin' your gear and ridin' out. For good, Slocum, for good."

"I don't take orders from you."

"Reckon not since Mr. Magnuson fired you, but if you still worked for the Bar M, you'd be doin' what I say."

Slocum stared at Garvin.

"That's right. I'm the new foreman. Tole you I'd get the job one day. It jist came sooner 'n I thought. From the look on your face, it came a hell of a lot sooner than you'd thought it would."

"You can't run a ranch this size."

"Can and will. And you got ten minutes to gather your shit and ride on out." Garvin squared his stance and curled his fingers around the butt of his six-gun.

"You going to throw down on me?" Slocum knew he was at a disadvantage sitting on the edge of the bunk, but not all that much since he had a cross-draw holster. The angle was more difficult for him, but he was quicker and a better shot than Tom Garvin.

"Not 'less you force me."

"You'd like that, wouldn't you? You got a taste of killing and can't get it out of your mouth."

"You was a friend, Slocum. Once. You thought you was helpin' me, but I see how you didn't do anything but hold me down. No more."

"Go to hell," Slocum said. He slid his saddlebags from under the bunk, slung them over his shoulder, and pushed past the new foreman of the Bar M Ranch.

The night seemed colder and less inviting than it should have as he saddled and rode from the spread.

16

"Slocum?"

Slocum didn't bother turning to see who called him. All he wanted to do was knock back yet another shot of the cheap whiskey. He had a goodly sum of money from his work at the Bar M but wanted to preserve as much as possible. The trade whiskey burned all the way down, punishing his gullet and belly, and he needed that. The bruises on his ribs burned, and the disgust he felt for Magnuson burned even brighter.

"Slocum!"

He finally half turned, winced at the pain in his side and saw Jed Blassingame a pace behind him. The man leaned heavily on a cane and looked half past dead. His weathered face had turned pale, and he moved like an old man.

"Buy you a drink?" Slocum offered.

"Can use one, but that's not what I wanted to ask. Let's set a spell. I can't get around the way I used to and standin' gives me pains."

Slocum had the barkeep pour another shot, which he carried to a nearby table, where Blassingame had already dropped heavily into a chair. The man looked even older as Slocum studied him. He pushed the shot glass across the table.

"You need this more 'n I do."

Blassingame eyed the drink, then shook his head.

"Dr. Abbey is givin' me some medicine. If I try drinkin', it makes me puke my guts out. Can't wait 'til I ain't swillin' that medicine shit."

Slocum retrieved his whiskey and sipped at it rather than downing it in a single gulp. Changing the way he drank made it seem as if he was able to drink more.

"Heard tell Garvin's foreman now."

Slocum nodded. He ran his finger around the rim of the glass, then licked it off his finger. It was both salty and dusty, but it gave the whiskey more body. Slocum hunted for ways to make it taste different every time and was running out.

"He know what he's doin'?"

"What's it to you? You aren't foreman any longer. You don't even work there."

"Mr. Magnuson did right by me. He's payin' my doctor bills and gave me damned near a year's salary since I'd worked for him so long."

"Not the same as sleeping in his daughter's bed," Slocum said.

"You're the one what'd know about that," Blassingame said coldly. "She never had a lick of sense. Lovely girl, but she'd spread for any stud who came along." Blassingame stared hard at Slocum, as if he wanted to anger him.

Slocum finished his whiskey and set the glass down with a sharp click on the table.

"One of us ought to go," Slocum said.

"I'll go, but hear me out. There's somethin' wrong 'bout Tom Garvin. I owe Mr. Magnuson for his kindness."

"Garvin has changed. That's all I know."

"You know more 'n that," Blassingame said. "The rope. That black rope he carries. You know about it."

"I don't know anything about it except he sleeps with the damned thing." Slocum took a deep breath, thought about how Garvin treated it, how it seemed hot sometimes and the way it had stretched longer than any rope should have when he rescued him from the muddy island in the middle of the river—

"You know it ain't a normal rope."

"I don't know anything of the sort."

"His luck is too good. You know that. I heard stories 'bout what's happened."

"Can't say his luck is all good. Fact is, he's had terrible things happen." Slocum remembered how Garvin had shot himself, how he had been in the middle of the stampede and had almost drowned.

"He gets a bit of good luck, but the bad is worse. Then the good luck saves him only for more bad to bedevil him. That's what you're thinking, isn't it?"

"True."

"I heard about that black rope. The Devil's Rope, it's called. It's got a curse on it. If he doesn't get rid of it, it'll destroy him."

"What's it to you?"

Blassingame licked his lips, studied the empty shot glass, then locked eyes with Slocum.

"I owe Mordecai Magnuson. That bad luck swirls around like a damned tornado and will suck up him and the entire Bar M. I don't want to see that."

"Tell Magnuson."

"Tried. That rope is pullin' the wool over his eyes, same as it is Garvin. Nuthin' good will come from havin' him and that rope in charge at the ranch."

Slocum snorted. He believed in things he could see. Garvin was a tenderfoot and got himself in trouble because he didn't know better. His luck had been good getting out of those spots, though there had to be more than a streak of good luck having a heart on the wrong side of his chest and walking away from a gunshot that would have killed most men.

But it had nothing to do with the rope.

"I still don't know why you're telling me any of this," Slocum said.

"She might be a slut, but you love her. I kin tell. She even has feelings for you. I kin see that, too. You might be 'bout the first to get that far with her."

Slocum's heart beat faster at the man's words. Then he said, "Doesn't matter any to me. Her pa said he'd shoot me if I poked around the ranch. Can't imagine what he'd do if he caught Christine and me together." He bit back the word "again." There wasn't any reason for Blassingame to know every damned thing that had happened.

"You got an iron hand. Might be that's what Miss Christine needs."

Slocum tried to get a handle on why he stayed around town. Magnuson had made it clear he wasn't welcome on the Bar M. If Christine heard he was still here, she might come to him and . . .

Slocum stopped kidding himself. Blassingame was right. She would move on to another man, probably Josh Norton from the way she had been cozying up to him at the square dance. From all he had heard about the young rancher, he would end up like putty in Christine's hands. She would mold him any way she wanted and probably hate him for being that way.

"I've got business," Slocum said.

"Think about it. I don't want Garvin ruinin' the Bar M or gettin' Mr. Magnuson into trouble." Blassingame cleared his throat and added, "Wouldn't be bad if you and Miss Christine got together either."

"There's nothing I can do. There's nothing I want to do." Slocum stood, looked at the defeated old foreman, then left the saloon. He stepped out into the dusty afternoon. The rains had gone and left the strong winds to suck up the moisture from the ground. When the last of the water evaporated, the dust began to swirl about.

He ought to ride on and forget Magnuson—and Christine. Somehow, what was logical and what he would have done five months earlier no longer mattered. If he wanted Christine, he had to fight for her. He wasn't afraid of her pa, but getting into a fight with Magnuson didn't do much to win Christine's heart. He had to soothe the ruffled feathers and convince the rancher of his honorable intentions toward his daughter.

Slocum wasn't much for making speeches, but he had to make the effort. For Christine, he would.

He mounted and rode slowly toward the Bar M as he worked out what he would say. Some things didn't make any sense to him. Using what Blassingame had said about the new foreman and his cursed rope wasn't going to get him past the front door. He needed some other wedge to get in a word or two.

By the time he stopped under the wooden arch with the Bar M brand on it, Slocum had decided fancy words were for lawyers and preachers. As a simple man, he had to speak simply. What he felt for Magnuson's daughter ought to be good enough.

He rode straight to the ranch house and waited out front for a minute or so to see if Magnuson came boiling out. Or if a shotgun blast cut him down. When nobody stirred, he climbed down and went to the door. For a moment he hesitated, then knocked loudly.

"Mr. Magnuson, I want to have words with you."

Only silence from inside greeted him. Slocum felt a letdown. He had spent the ride out to the Bar M going over the things he had to say about Christine—to Christine—and nobody answered. Turning to the bunkhouse, he stuck his head inside. Empty.

Stride long, he went to the barn and heard someone humming "Dixie." Slocum pushed open the door and saw Jonesy working to muck the stalls.

"You never struck me as the type to commit suicide," Jonesy said. He leaned on the shovel, wiped his sleeve across his forehead, and then straightened. "Ain't none of the folks here have anything good to say about you. Whatever you did musta been a dandy."

"Where's Magnuson?"

"He don't check in with me, but gossip has it he's over at the Norton spread."

"Christine?"

"Now, Slocum, you lookin' to get me into trouble tellin' tales?"

"Do you know or not?"

"Nope, don't. One thing I do know is that you'd better watch your back. Garvin's been whippin' himself up into a killing rage over you."

"Why?" This startled Slocum. "I don't have a bone to pick with him."

"He's got one to pick with you." Jonesy frowned and wiped his forehead again. "Mighty hot in here for this time of year. Guess all the shit is steamy hot."

"Where's Garvin?"

"You thinkin' on havin' it out with him? I'd steer clear of our new foreman, if I was you. But I ain't, and for that I'm happy as all get-out."

"He got a taste for blood when he saved Magnuson from being robbed," Slocum said, knowing the anger that had built in Garvin went back farther than that. He couldn't remember how he had cut down the two rustlers.

"Been practicin' with that iron of his. I'm no expert, but he's lookin' quick, mighty quick."

"It's Magnuson I need to speak with."

Jonesy leaned more heavily on the shovel, turned and spat, then said, "Ridin' with you was a pleasure, Slocum.

Wish you'd been made permanent foreman. You do things different from Jed but you get things done."

"Garvin doesn't know what he's doing," Slocum said.

"Your words, not mine, about my new foreman. Got to get back to work. Watch your back, Slocum, watch your back and be careful what you say."

Slocum didn't need such advice. He never looked for trouble, but it always managed to find him. Outside in the afternoon sun, he looked around. The corrals stood empty, the horses turned out to graze on the fields where the cattle had roamed only a few weeks earlier. A gunshot echoed from some distance away. Then another and another. The sound made Slocum think the same gun was being fired repeatedly. When no answering shot came, he suspected this was what Jonesy had warned him about.

Tom Garvin was out practicing with his Smith & Wesson.

There wasn't anything to gain by facing the foreman. He got to his horse and rode in the direction of the Norton ranch. What Magnuson had to say to the senior Norton wasn't a concern, but the younger Norton and Christine did give Slocum a touch of foreboding.

He rode down the road a piece and set off across country to cut several miles from the trip. If Christine had gone with her pa, they'd have taken a buggy. Riding fast enough, he might head them off before they reached the Norton house. Slocum should have asked Jonesy how long they'd been gone, but it hadn't entered his mind until this moment.

Crossing the broad meadow where the square dance had been held, he rode straight to the Norton ranch house and saw the buggy parked out back. He dropped to the ground and went to the door. Before he could knock, the door opened and the elder Norton stepped out.

"You get off my property. I don't want your like here," Norton said.

"Is Mr. Magnuson here? We have to talk."

"I'll get my hands here and throw you off, Slocum.

Mordecai told me what you did. I don't know why he didn't get the marshal to throw you in jail, but I'm not as kind-hearted."

The man was thirty years older than Slocum. Pushing him out of the way to find Magnuson would have been easy, but Slocum held back.

"I don't want trouble. Ask Mr. Magnuson to come out and—"

"And nothing. I warned you. If you're not on your horse and riding in ten seconds, you'll regret it!" Norton balled his hands into bony fists.

Slocum had no quarrel with the senior Norton. He backed off and mounted. Joshua Norton glared at him from the doorway. Not knowing what else to do, Slocum started for the road leading off the property, then slowed and felt his guts tumble over and over.

The buggy out back was gone.

While he and Norton had exchanged words, the Magnusons had sneaked away.

Slocum started for the road, then cut across country when he was out of sight of the ranch house. He put his heels to his horse's flanks and galloped to catch up with the buggy. To his surprise, he found it within minutes abandoned at the edge of a wooded area.

He started to call out, then bit back his words when he heard laughter coming from deeper in the copse. The trees provided a wooden screen that blocked direct vision. The thick undergrowth was cleared out along one path.

Slocum tethered his horse and took the trail deeper into the woods, then slowed and finally stopped when he heard the voices. Josh Norton Junior and Christine.

"Oh, Josh, you know just the right things to say. I love you so!"

Slocum tasted bile in his mouth. He took a few more steps so he could see into a clearing where a blanket had been laid on the ground. A picnic basket, untouched, had been placed to one side.

But on the blanket Christine leaned back, her knees up and her skirt teasingly slipping back down to expose her bare thighs—and more.

The younger Norton stood above her. His arousal was obvious.

"I'm so happy we'll be married soon, my dear," he said.

"There's no reason not to practice for the honeymoon," she said, pulling her skirt back even farther.

Norton dropped to his knees and moved forward into her inviting arms.

Slocum caught himself with his Colt half drawn. He slammed it all the way into his holster, not knowing who he would have shot. Turning, he left them to their lovemaking while his anger churned his gut and made him shake all over.

17

"Another?" the barkeep asked. The mustachioed man stood a ways back, as if Slocum would snap at him.

Slocum didn't blame him. For the past hour he had been trying to drown his sorrow and had done nothing but get madder and drunker. Mostly madder. Somehow everything he had seen that afternoon burned off the numbing effect whiskey usually had on him. Even the various cuts and bruises ached again, not dulled by the liquor.

"Why not? I need to drink faster maybe."

"You're doin' a good job of knockin' 'em back," the bartender said skeptically. "Five or six an hour will put you way ahead of the cowboys when they start pouring in."

"When's that?"

"Couple hours. It's four o'clock now."

Slocum stared into the shot glass and the drop of amber fluid remaining in its curved bottom. A few more would do him well before he got on the trail. There was nothing keeping him here now that he had found out that Jed Blassingame had been right about Christine. If the foreman had told him that earlier, Slocum might have beaten him to a bloody pulp, but seeing with his own eyes how she had dropped him in favor of Josh Norton rankled. Festered. Turned his guts to some ugly, evil swamp.

"One more and I'm out of town for good," Slocum said.

The barkeep poured at arm's length. His hand shook just enough to knock loose the solitary drop at the mouth of the bottle. When the drop splashed into the pool of whiskey in the glass, the man jumped back.

"Don't have a quarrel with you," Slocum said.

"Not you, Slocum," the barkeep said, going to the far end of the bar.

Slocum looked up and caught sight of the mirror behind the bar. His hand started for his six-shooter, but a strong hand on his shoulder stopped him from drawing.

"Wondered when you'd be around, Slocum," Pendergast said. His henchman, Herman, and another member of the gang positioned themselves behind Slocum. Trying to shoot it out now was out of the question.

"Didn't know you were looking for me."

"Of course I am. Why, we're good buddies, trail partners. No reason I shouldn't look for you to discuss our business." Pendergast looked up and caught the barkeep's eye. He motioned for another round.

"I don't want any more," Slocum said.

"Of course you do, Slocum," Pendergast said, his voice colder now. He took the drinks while his henchmen steered Slocum to a table. The outlaw put the liquor in front of Slocum. "Drink up."

Slocum knocked it back. This time it didn't soothe him but instead tore at his gut as if he had downed pure nitric acid.

"Now we got things to talk over, now that all the ranchers have their money in that cracker box of a bank. You ready to set a few sticks of dynamite on that wall so we can mosey on in tonight?"

Slocum remembered how he had been treated by Magnuson and Christine. He owed them nothing. If anything, getting even would set real pretty with him right now, but the other ranchers didn't deserve to have their year's earnings snatched from under them.

"I know what you're thinkin', Slocum. You're one of the decent types. A bit jagged around the edges, I do admit, but you're thinkin' how that money won't get into the right hands." Pendergast tipped back in his chair, leaning against the wall. "Isn't that so?"

Slocum said nothing.

"All the cowboys been paid. The men who actually do the work have money jinglin' in their pockets. Like you. In spite of what Magnuson did to you, you got paid. Right?"

"He paid me," Slocum said carefully. "It wasn't what he owed me."

"Exactly! He owed you a powerful lot more. He owed you for the danger out there on the drive, and for you ramroddin' the herd through for him. Instead, he came damned near to tarrin' and featherin' you. Don't tell me that's not so."

"It's true."

"And he gave the foreman's job to a cowboy who's still wet behind the ears. Let's say Magnuson kept his money and that boy ran his ranch next year. What do you think would happen? Well, sir, I'll tell you. Magnuson would lose his entire investment because his foreman didn't know one end of a gun from the other."

"You heard?"

"Heard? Every damned soul in town's heard how Garvin upped and shot himself. You tried to show him what's right, and he betrayed you. He turned on you like a rabid dog. A man who's so dumb he'd shoot himself betrayed you and took the job that by rights should have gone to you."

"You ought to have been a lawyer. You're making a mighty fine case for me helping you."

"This won't be anything you haven't done before," Pendergast said. "Now my boys, they're the tenderfoots when it comes to bank robbin'. A better bunch you couldn't pick for rustling cattle, but this is a new profession for them. You're the expert. You're the one we have to rely on."

"You've robbed a bank or two yourself," Slocum said. "Probably stagecoaches, too."

"And, I do admit, a train. Just one, mind you, but it was an experience that would have been made better if someone skilled in the art had been there to help me."

"Like you want me to be to rob the bank."

"Four a.m. strikes me as a good time. We'll all gather by that wall. My boys'll have sacks ready for the money."

"And the explosive?"

"I got that. Blasting caps and fuse, too."

Slocum hesitated. It was more than Magnuson's money in that bank. More than Norton's. At least three other ranchers had their yearly profit sitting there, waiting to be used over the winter to buy supplies and in the spring to get new herds together.

"How long?"

"What?" Slocum stared at Pendergast and the sly look on his face.

"How long should the fuse be?"

"A foot or two. Burns a foot a minute if you got the right miner's fuse."

"Then we're in business. You're the one we need, Slocum, and by sunup we're all gonna be filthy rich. Where you thinkin' on runnin'? After we get ourselves rich?"

Slocum hadn't considered that he'd have the law on his trail. Simply riding from town was a lot different from having a determined marshal and furious ranchers coming after them.

"Hadn't thought on the matter," he said.

"You can ride with us. We make a good team, Slocum, you and me and Herman and Abe and all the rest. You know Herman. Abe's the one with the perpetual scowl on his face and the scars on both cheeks. He was prisoner of the Ute longer 'n he'd've liked. Since it's goin' to be winter soon enough, maybe we ought to ride south to Mexico and find ourselves purty señoritas to set on our knees while we're swillin' tequila and pulque. Me, I prefer pulque. How about you?"

Slocum realized how cleverly Pendergast kept pulling him into the robbery by holding out fantasies about Mexico and lovely, willing women far from the pursuing law. Never give him time to think about saying no and always keep him focused on what to do with the easy money from the robbery.

"We shouldn't be seen together anymore," Slocum said.

"You are a cautious one, Slocum. That's another thing I like about you." Pendergast stood and looked down at him. He touched the brim of his hat with the rattlesnake hide band. It buzzed just a little like a rattler. Slocum saw the tail that had been chopped off the snake once sporting the skin. It was eight or nine rattles long.

Slocum reminded himself of the difference between the rattler and Pendergast. The snake gave warning before striking.

"You like the addition to my hatband? Found a six-foot snake all curled up next to me the other morning. Killed it with my bare hands and took its rattles. Bit 'em off, I did. Didn't even use a knife." Pendergast laughed. Slocum wasn't sure if any of it was true, but it made a good story. And it again diverted him from finding reasons to walk away from robbing the Central City Bank.

Pendergast slapped him on the shoulder, then he and his men left Slocum sitting at the table, staring after them. He had considered simply riding on and to hell with Magnuson— and Christine—but Pendergast and his silver tongue had swayed him. The best way he could punish the rancher was to steal his money.

Such thievery as bank robbing didn't worry Slocum unduly. When the need had arisen, he had done worse in the past. But that wasn't really how he wanted to punish Mordecai Magnuson.

And having any dealings with Pendergast would be deadly. The man had trailed him for the better part of a year to get even with him. Why was he so willing to welcome Slocum into his gang after such a chase?

"Sidewinders don't have rattles," he said.

"How's that, Slocum?" The barkeep came to the end of the bar and leaned over. "You wantin' somethin'?"

"I'm done," Slocum said. He stepped outside and let the cool air wash over him and give added purpose to what he knew he had to do.

Wary of any of the gang spying on him, he wandered about town awhile, slowed, and went to the wall he had chosen to blow down to reach the vault, then sat for a spell and waited. If Pendergast or any of his henchmen trailed him, they were doing a fine job. Slocum saw a few citizens milling about, then disappear as they went home for dinner. The sun dipped low and the temperature dropped fast with it.

Only when he was sure no one watched him did he go toward the marshal's office. If the lawman had a half-dozen deputies lying in wait, he could snare Pendergast and his entire gang when they showed up for the robbery. He'd have to do some convincing of his own to make the marshal believe the bank was going to be robbed, but that wasn't too hard since the marshal kept his job by staying in the surrounding ranchers' good graces. Anything threatening their livelihood was bad for him keeping his job.

He circled the block and came up to the jailhouse from behind. A single light shone through the barred window high on one adobe wall. Whether the marshal had a prisoner or this was just a lamp left burning hardly mattered. It would take a few minutes to lay out Pendergast's plan and then—

Something moved to Slocum's right. He turned and his hand flashed to the Colt in its cross-draw holster. The six-shooter came all the way out and then slipped from his fingers. The distraction to his right had been a decoy and nothing more. The real attack came from behind. A heavy weight descended on his head and drove him to his knees. He fumbled to grab his six-gun, now on the ground in front of him.

A second blow put him out like a light.

Pain woke him. Slocum thought he had been out for only a few seconds, but the town had gone away and was replaced by a barn. He caught the deep scent of horses and heard chickens stirring, making him think it was close to dawn.

A moment of panic seized him when he definitely heard a cock crow. Pendergast would have already robbed the bank and would be riding away. He had threatened to make life hell for Slocum if he didn't set the charges for the gang. What might he have done if Slocum was nowhere to be seen?

The pain doubled as Slocum began to struggle. He looked up and saw his hands were securely bound to a beam. Pulled up so his toes barely touched the floor, he felt muscles begin to protest. His belly and legs and across his shoulders—all burned as if he had been set on fire.

"He's awake." The words came from a long way off. Slocum heard footsteps approaching. The men had been outside the barn.

He tried to swing around to see who had come into the barn but was stopped with a short, hard punch to the kidneys that caused his world to turn black again for a moment. Gasping, he forced himself to focus his eyes. He expected to see Pendergast. To his surprise, Josh Norton and a cowboy he had never seen before stood in front of him. The young rancher balled his hand and held it up under Slocum's nose.

"You keep quiet, or I'll hit you again."

"Want me to gag him, Josh?"

"This is all right," Norton said. He walked behind Slocum and punched him again.

This time Slocum was ready for the blow, but it still hurt like hell.

"That the best you can do? Beat on a man you've got tied up?"

Norton hit him again, this time too high to smash into the kidneys. Slocum winced because his ribs were still bruised from Magnuson kicking the hell out of him, but this blow was endurable.

"You want to say something or just walk around punching a helpless man?" Slocum asked.

"I told you to shut up!" Norton's voice cracked and broke. Slocum couldn't tell if it came from strain or simple adolescent growth. He doubted Josh Junior shaved more than a couple times a week.

"Josh, we can't keep him here forever," the cowboy said uneasily. "You know why."

"We shoulda tied him up out in the woods." He slugged Slocum again, but he also grunted, as if the punch hurt his fist more than it did his target.

Norton walked back around and stepped truculently close to Slocum.

"You got fired over on the Bar M. You're still around. I want you to get out of the county. I don't ever want to see your ugly face here again."

"How's Christine?" Slocum's jibe caused Norton to turn red in the face.

"I want you to leave her alone, and I swear, I'll kill you if you don't get out of here!"

"Wouldn't be hard to kill me right now," Slocum said, "and it's hard for me to leave when you got me strung up like a side of beef."

Norton cocked his fist back to hit Slocum again, but he checked himself at the last instant.

"I didn't bring you here to bandy words, Slocum. This is a warning. A *friendly* warning compared to what I'll do if you don't leave."

"You got the balls to kill a man?"

"Yes!"

Slocum looked past Norton and his henchman to a side door. The elder Norton stepped through and paused, taking in what he saw.

"You don't have the gumption. You going to have your old man kill me for you?"

"He's an old fool! He doesn't understand. I'll kill you, Slocum, I will!"

"Junior." The single word came low and cold. It froze the younger Norton.

Slocum didn't even try to keep from laughing at the way Junior blanched.

"What's going on?" The older Norton came over.

"Sir, I—"

"Get out of here, Ashe. This is a family matter."

The cowboy mumbled an apology and disappeared behind Slocum, leaving the two Nortons and Slocum alone with the horses.

"You've got two choices, Norton," Slocum said. "Kill me while I'm all strung up or let me go."

"He'll kill us, Pa!"

"Shut up," Norton said, not even looking at his son. "You've made a mess of this."

"I'm not letting him have Christine! I love her!"

"I said to shut up." Norton backhanded his son, sending him crashing into a stall. The horse neighed and kicked back. Norton came over and looked at Slocum for a few seconds before he said, "He rough you up much?"

"Had worse done to me."

"Should I kill you?"

"Can't stop you if you try."

"What if I cut you down and tell you to get the hell out of here?"

"You can do that, too."

"Would you leave?"

Slocum considered his options. He didn't want to die, but he wasn't backing down either.

"If I want to. Fact was, I was on my way out of town when he and Ashe waylaid me."

"That true, Junior?"

"Pa, he—"

"Was he leaving town?"

"Don't know. He was going to the marshal's office."

"Why were you going to see Marshal Swearingen?"

"Heard tell there was going to be a bank robbery and wanted him to know."

"Who? You? You were going to rob the bank?"

"A man who has it in for me by the name of Wiley Pendergast. He tried to lure me into it, but I wouldn't go along."

Norton snorted and shook his head.

"Can't see you as an honest man, Slocum."

Slocum said nothing.

"When was this supposed to happen?"

"Just before dawn."

"So," said Norton, "if you're telling the truth, the bank's been robbed."

"While your son had me all trussed up so he could beat on me," Slocum said.

"Ashe!" Norton bellowed again and brought the cowboy running. "Keep Slocum tied up. We're going into town. All of us. If he's lied to me, I'll see to cleaning up your mess, Junior."

"I'm not lying," Slocum said.

"Then I'll tend to my own without your help, Slocum." Norton glared at his son, then motioned for Ashe to bring Slocum along.

18

As they rode into town, Slocum heard the tumult before he saw the citizens running around, waving their fists and shrilly insisting that Marshal Swearingen do something. Slocum had heard such demands before, always from frightened, angry men with no idea what to do—but something had to be done quick. Especially if the man they demanded action from was a mayor or a marshal.

"What's going on, Pa?" Josh Norton stood in the stirrups as he looked down the main street.

"How the hell should I know?" his pa said sourly. "I just got here, like you."

"Slocum?" The younger Norton turned to their prisoner. "What kind of trouble have you caused?"

"You've got me all tied up," Slocum said, holding his bound wrists up for the boy to see. "You slugged me a bit after midnight, and you haven't let me out of your sight since."

"Still doesn't mean this isn't your doing."

"Was there any ruckus when you cold-cocked me?"

"No," said Norton, working this over. "That doesn't mean—"

"Shut up, Junior," the elder Norton said sharply. "Slocum's right. Whatever's got 'em all stirred up like pouring boiling water down an anthill's not his doing."

They rode forward. As the townspeople spied Slocum, they fell silent, then formed behind like a parade, making him uneasy. They whispered among themselves now. Ugly whispers. Uglier looks. He felt a lynch mob building around him like a lightning-filled thunderstorm, and there wasn't a damned thing he could do about it.

"You takin' him to the marshal, Mr. Norton?" someone in the crowd called.

"Reckon so."

"Give 'im over to us, and we'll see he gets the justice he deserves!"

Slocum began looking for some way to escape—but didn't see it. The crowd all around him could easily pull him from his horse, no matter how he urged it to a gallop. Some of the men fingered six-shooters and others sent their womenfolk back to stores and houses. That never boded well.

"Mr. Norton, you done caught the son of a bitch."

"Morning, Marshal. What's going on?"

"The bank was robbed and that owlhoot was one of the robbers."

"When was it robbed?"

"You shut up, Slocum. You know damn well you robbed it just as it opened," the marshal said.

"Around nine?" Slocum asked.

"Nine," confirmed someone in the crowd. "And we got witnesses to you killin' all them."

Slocum's mind raced. Pendergast hadn't blown down the wall to rifle the vault. Instead, he had bulled his way in after Roebuck opened for the day. From the sound of "killin' all them," Pendergast hadn't minded spraying lead about liberally. That matched what Slocum thought of him.

"How do you know it was Slocum?" Norton asked.

"One of them robbers kept shouting his name. Every time he shouted 'Slocum,' somebody died."

The crowd roared in agreement and eager hands pulled Slocum from the saddle. He hit the ground, only to be dragged along, his toes leaving twin furrows in the dirt.

"There's a beam high enough in front of the saloon," somebody cried. "Get a rope!"

The crowd's mood was turning more bloodthirsty by the minute. Slocum struggled but could not hope to escape. His mind raced on ways to avoid getting his neck stretched.

Nothing came to him as a chair was placed under the exposed beam and a rope was tossed over it to swing ominously to and fro.

"Wait, hold your horses!" The barkeep came boiling out from the saloon, waving his shotgun around. "You cain't hang him here. Not in front of my saloon!"

"Git on back. He done kilt three men and robbed the bank."

The barkeep stepped back. For a moment Slocum dared hope the man would intervene, but he seemed to be tossed on the horns of a dilemma. One way let Slocum hang. The other put him in the sights of an angry mob of his neighbors.

"Nobody's hangin' him." The marshal punctuated his order with a shot fired into the air. "That's not the way the law works. First we try him, then we hang him!"

"We kin save a passel of time by hangin' him now."

Slocum was shoved onto the chair and the rope brought to his head.

A second shot rang out. The time the voice wasn't that of Marshal Swearingen but Josh Norton.

"You boys back off," the rancher said, moving to put himself between Slocum and the lynch mob. "I want some more information 'fore I let you execute him."

"What's to tell? He done stole *your* money, Josh."

"Somebody did, but why do you think it was Slocum's doing?"

"I heard the leader shout his name. He barely said the name, and Slocum'd shoot another of my tellers." The bank president forced his way through the crowd.

"How'd you keep from getting killed?" Josh Norton asked.

"Danged lucky. I hid under my desk whilst they were shootin' my employees! There wasn't any other way to get away alive from that murderous swine."

"You saw Slocum?"

"The one leadin' 'em called his name. But they all wore masks."

"Look at what Slocum's wearing," Norton said. "That match up with the owlhoot doing the killing?"

"Well, no. And the man shootin' my tellers was taller, a lot taller."

Slocum knew who that was. Herman. Pendergast had told his right-hand man to kill if he shouted the name "Slocum" to give the impression he had been along. This was the way Pendergast intended to pay him back for not showing up to set the dynamite—or maybe this was what Pendergast had intended all along. The man had trailed him for so long that Slocum found it hard to believe he'd give up a grudge easily.

"What horse was Slocum riding? That one?" Norton pointed to the horse back by the marshal's office.

"Naw, it was a gray. But he could have switched horses. And changed clothes. How come you brought him in, Josh, if not for the robbery?" Roebuck moved even closer, squinting at Slocum and sniffing. "He doesn't smell the same either. The one called Slocum smelled of peppermint. You don't wash that off easily. But he could, I reckon."

"He hasn't changed clothes or scrubbed himself clean, not since midnight last night." Norton looked at his son, then at Slocum, before turning back to the crowd. "He was my guest and either me or my son was with him the whole time. Out at my ranch, not here in town."

"Where were you at nine?" Roebuck asked.

"We were riding into town. Ashe and Junior were

alongside the whole way. Slocum'd have to be in two places at once, 'less you got the time wrong."

"No, I don't. Lots of others in town saw the getaway."

"It was a little after nine." The agreement spread through the crowd.

"But why'd they want to call out his name during the robbery, if he weren't one of the gang?"

"I think I kin answer that," the barkeep said. He pushed to stand beside Norton. "Last night, right around twilight, a hard-looking gent bought Slocum a drink. One of his partners answers the description of the man what done the killing."

"Who was it, Slocum? Who bought you a drink?"

"His name's Pendergast." Slocum's mind raced. "He's had it in for me ever since I did him dirt back in California. He's followed me for the last year. Longer."

"Mighty convenient," a man in front muttered.

"He wears a hat with a snake hatband and a rattler's tail fastened to it. If he shakes his head, it sounds like a rattlesnake fixing to strike."

"The leader," Roebuck said loudly. "He wore such a hatband."

"I seen that hatband, too," the barkeep said. "Made me uneasy the way this Pendergast fellow kept tossin' his head from side to side to make it rattle."

"Just knowing a bank robber don't make him one," Marshal Swearingen said, moving closer to where Slocum stood precariously on the chair. The rope kept blowing into his face. "Let him down."

To Slocum's surprise, Mordecai Magnuson came up along the boardwalk and spoke. "You vouch for him, Josh?"

"I do."

"I know you don't have any more liking for him than I do, but if you say he couldn't have done the robbery, Josh, that's good enough for me. Let him down. Cut those ropes off his hands." Magnuson pointed and men jumped to obey.

Slocum stepped down and rubbed his wrists after the ropes had been removed. He knew Magnuson's reason for speaking up—because Norton had. His future in-law wasn't to be crossed in the matter.

The two men stepped back and talked while the crowd stirred about uneasily. Slocum overheard them mention Josh Junior and Christine's nuptials, their mutual loss from the bank robbery—and Slocum. He didn't like that neither man had anything too good to say about him, but he respected them for sticking up for him when it would have been simple to turn their backs and let the lynch mob have its way.

They beckoned to the marshal, and he joined them in earnest conversation. Swearingen nodded as if his head were mounted on a spring, then he went back to face the crowd.

"There's a hundred-dollar reward for the capture of the varmints what robbed the bank."

"Two hundred," Magnuson called. "A hundred from each of us, me and Josh Norton."

The ripple of interest went through the crowd. Slocum heaved a sigh of relief since lust for money had replaced bloodlust. His neck still itched from the nearness of the noose.

"What's the leader's name, Slocum?" The marshal cut the ropes on his hands. "What did you say it was? The one with the rattlesnake skin hatband?"

"Wiley Pendergast. He's got a couple men with him named Abe and Herman."

"Ain't much help, but might be when we catch up with them. I'm formin' up a posse to go after 'em. Who's with me?"

A dozen men in the crowd cheered and began forcing their way to the front. Slocum stepped to one side to figure out what he ought to do.

"I got my men on their trail already," Magnuson said.

"Garvin's leading them?" Slocum asked. Magnuson only glared at him, but this was answer enough. The young cowboy was going up against a hardened outlaw and his gang.

That didn't strike Slocum as likely to turn out very well, but Garvin had wanted to shoot first and ask questions later for a spell.

He had to shoot first in a half-dozen instances—Pendergast and all his gang—if he wanted to stay alive.

"You want me to ride along?" Slocum asked. The words slipped from his mouth before he had a chance to think.

"I want you the hell away from me and mine," Magnuson said.

"Yeah, just forget what's happened and move on," Norton said, more uneasily. It didn't set well with him how his son had tried to scare off Slocum; he wasn't going to bring out the dirty laundry for everyone to see.

The two ranchers went off, shoulder to shoulder and deep in conversation. The marshal gathered his posse and ordered them to assemble at the jailhouse so they could plan for the pursuit. To Slocum's way of thinking, the marshal was a day late and a dollar short. The posse ought to have been on the outlaws' trail hours earlier.

Mostly, he wasn't offering advice. He was just happy to be alive after the run-in with the mob.

"Buy you a drink, Slocum. You can use it." The barkeep looked at his fellow citizens and shook his head.

Slocum went into the saloon and let the barkeep set him up with a drink. He savored it rather than knocking it back. Every drop was more precious now than ever before. The brush with getting his neck stretched did that to him.

"I ought to be buying you the drink," Slocum said. "You pulled my fat from the fire."

"I hate mobs," the barkeep said with surprising loathing in his voice. Slocum wondered if he had been the guest of honor at a necktie party. "The more there are, the dumber they get. Still, it was good you and Norton were together and that he spoke up when he did."

"Never thought getting the shit kicked out of me would be a good thing."

"Junior?" The barkeep nodded as he read Slocum's expression. "He don't have a lick of sense. Heard about how Magnuson is marryin' off his daughter to him. That boy's never gonna have a moment's peace. She'll wear the pants in that family. When she bothers to wear anything at all."

Slocum bristled, then finished his drink. He had no reason to defend Christine's reputation. For all he knew, it was well deserved, but that didn't affect the way he thought of her. Most of the women he had found traveling the West had gotten what they wanted, usually through sex. It hadn't seemed Christine was that way, not with him, though he didn't mind the lovemaking with her one bit, but the townspeople saw her differently. He might have avoided some real heartbreak since they obviously knew her better than he did.

"She never would have, Slocum."

"What's that?"

"Married you. Don't get your dander up, but the way you get all doe-eyed when you think of her tells me 'bout everything I need to know. She's had her cap set for young Norton for a while. Might be her and her pa have since the Norton spread's twice the size of the Bar M. The pair of them wouldn't care if you were the hardest-working cowboy this side of the Mississippi. How much the coin jingled in your pocket would always matter more."

"Might be I should count myself lucky."

"You were. Have another, then that's it. I gotta make a profit here some way." The bartender poured out the drink. Again Slocum sipped at it, letting it burn his lips and then wash around in his mouth before plunging down his gullet to warm his belly.

"You see Pendergast after he left me last night?"

"You dodged one bullet with Miss Christine. Don't go puttin' yourself in front of a damned firin' squad."

"Pendergast," he insisted. "You see him or his men again?"

"Nope. From the way he threw his weight around, I'd have known."

Slocum considered the robbery from all directions. Pendergast had intended to frame him for the robbery if he hadn't taken part. If he had agreed to blow open the wall, there might have been an unfortunate accident with a stick of dynamite that would've left him dead at the scene. Either way was fine with Pendergast.

"Stayin' in town don't look like much of a future for you," the barkeep said. "I could use a bouncer, but not you. Leave. Ride out. Choose your direction, but get out of here. That's better for you than a third free drink."

"Don't expect me to go looking to collect that reward," Slocum said.

"You wouldn't have much chance at it."

"The posse?"

The bartender snorted contemptuously and said, "Roebuck sent telegrams all over offerin' a reward. By now every bounty hunter in a hundred miles is huntin' down Pendergast and his boys."

Slocum considered this. Competition didn't bother him none. He'd find Pendergast and his men, but it wouldn't be to collect the reward. The best Slocum could do after getting even with the outlaw leader was to take the spoils from the bank robbery. That seemed little enough recompense for all he had been through. His fingers traced out the bruises left by Magnuson's boot and then the tender spots above his kidneys where Josh Junior had used him as a punching bag. He had been set up as a scapegoat and used by about everybody. Magnuson and Norton had alibied him, but telling the truth wasn't something that deserved to be rewarded. A man told the truth, no matter what.

The money from the bank robbery would hardly be enough to pay him back, even after he got Pendergast in his gun sight. He made sure there wasn't a drop left in the shot glass and then he left the saloon without a look back. Slocum had some tracking ahead of him, dangerous tracking.

19

Slocum didn't bother following the road the way the posse had gone. Pendergast wasn't stupid enough to stay on a main road very long, even if he had left mounts along the way Pony Express style to get the hell out of the territory in a day's time. From what Slocum had seen, Pendergast's gang rode a single horse. They might have stolen enough for a relay, but none of the ranchers had mentioned losing that many of their remuda after the cattle drive.

He cut across country, found a spot that looked likely where a foot-deep stream ran, and rode alongside. Eyes peeled for any trace that Pendergast and his men had come this way, Slocum finally spotted a single hoofprint in the muddy embankment. He rode up to a rise and got his bearings. This wasn't far from where Pendergast and Herman had brought him before. Their camp wouldn't be too far, but he knew it would be abandoned.

It took him almost an hour but he found where they had tried to hide several campfires by throwing rocks and dirt over them, then dropping dead limbs and branches. A slow circuit convinced him this had been Pendergast's campsite.

Three sets of tracks left the camp, each heading in a different direction away from town. The gang had split their take and now rode away to find someplace to spend the money.

Any of the tracks could belong to Pendergast. Slocum closed his eyes and sat for a minute or longer, trying to remember anything the outlaw leader might have said about a hideout. He was nothing if not careful, that Pendergast. If he had mentioned a spot, Slocum hadn't heard or understood. More likely, the outlaw hadn't mentioned it. After all, he intended for Slocum to die one way or the other after the robbery.

Would he have come back to town for the execution if Slocum had been caught and convicted of multiple murder? It was likely. That might mean he hadn't gone too far. After all, Pendergast wasn't aware that his distinctive hatband had given away his identity and might think he was secure in returning to gloat.

Slocum picked a track and chased after the riders, from the look of the prints, numbering only two. He trotted along, working to keep the hoofprints in sight. Once they got to the far side of the meadow, the prints vanished in a welter of leaves and detritus in an overgrown wood. There hadn't been any evidence the outlaws were trying to lay a false trail or even hide their direction of travel. Slocum pushed on hard, making his way through the forest as quickly as he could.

How far ahead they were, he couldn't guess, but he had the feeling they weren't in any big hurry. Moving in a straight line, he eventually crossed a level stretch and worked his way to a rise where he could survey a couple miles farther. He didn't even have to use his field glasses to see the two riders. They rode slowly, not bothering to look around.

A quick judgment as to their destination sent him in a long arc that circled into a muddy ravine and then up a distant hill that brought him even with them two.

He slid his Colt Navy from its holster and leveled it,

waiting. As they rode up and crested the hill, they saw him—and his six-shooter.

"Howdy," he said. "You've been busy since Pendergast left me last night."

Herman went for his six-gun, but he wore it on his right hip, high, and had to twist around to get it out. Slocum's bullet caught him in the leg. The wound wasn't serious, but it caused his horse to rear, throwing the outlaw.

The other outlaw, the scarred one Pendergast had called Abe, bent forward and pulled out his rifle for some serious shooting. Slocum knew better than to shoot it out with a man sighting in on him with a rifle. He fired a couple more times at the horse's hooves, causing it to dance about and spoiling Abe's aim long enough to take cover.

He had been too eager to confront the outlaws. Worse, he had believed Pendergast would be one of the two riders. If he had scouted more, spied on them, and waited for them to camp before going after them, he wouldn't be worrying about Abe getting lucky with a shot.

High-powered rifle slugs whined through the air. Slocum grabbed for his own rifle but his horse was as skittish as Abe's. He dismounted and held on to the reins, but Abe wasn't anyone's fool. He knew that attack served him better than defense and came rushing over the hill, firing as he came.

Slocum had to abandon his horse and depend on his six-shooter. He got off a couple shots that convinced Abe to flop belly down on the ground and take more care aiming.

"That you, Slocum? You son of a bitch. Why won't you die!"

"That's what Pendergast wanted for me, isn't it?"

"Where'd you go last night? We was gonna blow the wall down, but you turned tail and ran."

Slocum worked to reload, looking for his chance to stop Abe.

"Pendergast would have shot me down like a dog," Slocum said. "Why help rob the bank if I was going to end up dead?"

Abe laughed harshly.

"You got it all wrong, Slocum. The boss is a straight shooter. He woulda given you your fair share. Hell, me and Herman will share what we got. Only seems fair, and we got a shitload of money from that hick town bank."

"That's mighty generous," Slocum said, working his way to a fallen log. He kept low, wiggled like a snake, and came up behind. If Abe had seen him, he didn't take a shot.

"That's us, Slocum. Real generous. What do you say? Let's call a truce and divvy the money."

Slocum stayed silent and judged where Abe had to go if he continued his frontal attack. He rested his Colt on the top of the log to steady his aim.

"Slocum? What do you say?"

He said nothing. Abe would get antsy and make a mistake.

"Slocum? Slocum! I'm comin' out."

The outlaw held his rifle high over his head with both hands and worked his way toward the spot where Slocum had originally hidden.

"See, Slocum? I'm comin' out. You all right? I didn't hit you, did I? Let me help."

Abe stopped, looking off at an angle from where Slocum lay.

"Drop the rifle," Slocum called. He should have cut the outlaw down where he stood, but Abe had his hands in the air. "Drop it or you're a dead man."

Abe jerked around, surprise on his face.

"How'd you get over there? Don't shoot! I'm settin' down my rifle." Abe turned as if dipped in molasses, his every move exaggerated and slow. He rested his rifle against a rock and put his hands back up. "Come on, Slocum. We don't have to be like this. We can ride together."

"Where's Pendergast?"

"To hell with Pendergast. He's always bossin' me around. Let's the two of us ride together. Partners. You got imagination. We can do some great robberies, and not just banks. Trains, stagecoaches. Hell, we can hit cavalry payrolls."

"You've got some ambition," Slocum said, standing and advancing on Abe, his six-shooter never moving from the man. The slightest twitch and the outlaw would die, but he seemed content to talk his nonsense. There was no reason in hell Abe would want to partner with him.

"We can be partners, Slocum. Partners." Abe turned slightly, and Slocum caught the glint of light off metal.

His finger came back fast, jerking his aim a little off target. He still hit Abe high in the chest, causing the owlhoot to spin, grab for his rifle, and crash to the ground. Behind him, prone on the ground, lay Herman. Slocum hadn't winged him as bad as he'd thought. The two road agents worked together well. There hadn't been any need for them to make lengthy plans to lay the ambush.

Slocum fired as he walked forward. Herman grunted, returned fire, then died with the last of Slocum's bullets ripping through the crown of his hat and blowing his brains into bloody mush.

"You kilt him! You kilt Herman!"

Slocum bent double, got his feet under him, and dived parallel to the ground as Abe opened fire with his rifle.

He landed hard, rolled downhill, and avoided the hail of bullets sent his way. After skidding to a halt, he dug his toes into the soft ground and looked uphill. He cursed when he had a good shot at Abe—but his six-gun was empty.

He reloaded and found he didn't have enough for a full cylinder. Four shots. That was all he had to eliminate Abe, but killing the man wasn't his intent. The gang had a rendezvous point, those who wanted to continue riding with Pendergast. Slocum wanted to be there to settle the score with their leader.

He rolled and kept rolling, sliding downhill a little.

"Want me, come and get me, Abe."

His only reply was a half-dozen rounds. Slocum wondered

if the outlaw was running dry like he was. He clutched the ebony butt of his six-gun and pictured the four rounds resting in the chambers. He got to the base of the hill and looked for a spot to make his stand—or better, to lay a trap. He didn't know how badly injured Abe was, but if he and Herman had been partners, his anger might propel him forward, no matter how much lead he carried in his body.

Not finding any decent cover, Slocum kept running. No bullets. There were too many possibilities why Abe failed to take a shot at him. Out of ammo was one, but Slocum had to discount that. It would be too easy to rush the wounded outlaw and find himself with a gut full of lead. Abe might be pinned down where he was because of wounds. That wasn't a chance Slocum wanted to take either. Better to think Abe was moving around, had a magazine full of rounds, and bided his time for the killing shot.

The base of the hill proved slippery from the recent rain. The runoff had poured down the hillside and carried away both debris and dirt. Slocum smiled when he saw one deeply cut ravine. This was what he needed. It was filthy work, flopping belly down and wiggling uphill in the muddy-bottomed arroyo, but he was protected from fire.

At least he thought he was. He made it halfway up the hill when he looked up and saw Abe bracing himself against a tree, his rifle to his shoulder.

"Figgered you'd be comin' this way, Slocum." He snugged the rifle stock to his shoulder.

Slocum fired. The shot went wild but startled Abe enough for him to jerk on the trigger. The shot flew high. Scrambling frantically to get his feet under him proved too difficult for Slocum. He fell facedown in the mud. Another round whined harmlessly above him.

Slocum couldn't advance; retreat was suicidal. All he could do was make his final three shots count. Two missed, the third caught Abe as he stepped away from the tree to get a better field of fire.

"Oh," Abe said, then sat down. He weakly lifted the rifle, but it slipped from his shoulder as he kneeled over.

Slocum rolled from the ravine and found drier ground to get back to the top of the hill. Abe lay on his side, his hands between his legs, which were drawn up to his chest. In this fetal position, no wound was obvious. Slocum considered how he had felt with the last shot.

Over the years he had developed a sense of when a shot was good and when it missed. Reliving the moment he pulled the trigger on his fourth and final round convinced him his shot hadn't ended Abe's life. He still advanced with his empty six-gun pointed at the fallen outlaw.

"You're playing possum," Slocum said.

"You're right, Slocum, I am!" Abe rolled over. In a flash Slocum saw where two bullets had entered the man's chest, both high and painful but not fatal. More than this, he saw a derringer clutched in Abe's hand.

He thrust out his arm, pointing his empty six-shooter at Abe.

"I don't want to kill you, but I got a better chance of ending your miserable life than you do ending mine." Slocum's hand was steady as a rock. Abe's shook.

"You kilt Herman and shot me twice."

"I want to know where to find Pendergast. He's the one I'm after, not you."

"Y-You'd let me go?" The small pistol shook even more. If Slocum had had any rounds left, he would have shot Abe dead rather than take the chance the man would jerk and fire accidentally.

"Yeah, I'd do that."

"Why?"

"Pendergast told you how he's chased me down for over a year. You know he tried to frame me for the bank robbery and the murder of the tellers."

"Herman shot 'em."

"I know. He's paid for that crime. All you've done is rob

a bank, and I don't give a tin-plated damn about that. Where were you supposed to meet up with Pendergast?"

"He didn't give us our entire cut. Just some." Abe's arm sank and the derringer pointed more at Slocum's boots than his head.

"Keep your money. Keep Herman's cut, too, for all I care. The only way I can stop Pendergast from dogging my steps and making life hell is to kill him."

"You want to kill him? He's a son of a bitch but . . . but we done some good robberies. Smart as a fox." Abe's voice trailed off. Slocum didn't move a muscle.

Abe jerked back. His wounds were finally bleeding him dry, weakening him. He used both hands to hold the .45 derringer now. The muzzle looked as big as the maw of hell to Slocum, and then Abe's hands were unable to hold the pistol. It slipped from his hands to the ground.

Slocum stepped up, grabbed the derringer, and tucked it into his gun belt.

"Where's Pendergast?"

Abe's eyelids flickered.

"You know him. Always thinkin' of how to get away. Ain't gonna tell you how, not possible with all this rain swellin' . . ."

Slocum didn't have to check. Abe was dead.

As he buried both outlaws, he thought about what Abe said. Abe had thought he was taunting his killer with a vague statement, but the life draining from him had betrayed him. He had given Slocum one clue too many.

Slocum found the pitiful few dollars in the outlaws' saddlebags from the robbery. Pendergast had kept the bulk of it for himself or intended using it to ensure his gang would rendezvous if they wanted their share.

Which it was didn't matter. Slocum tucked the money into his own saddlebags, reloaded his Colt Navy, and then mounted for a long ride. He knew where to find Pendergast. And then he would kill him.

20

The road carried hoofprints of too many horses for him to be following only Pendergast. Slocum rode faster when he heard the bull-throated rush of the river. From here Pendergast must have thought to get on a riverboat and go downstream far enough to spend the money from the robbery in peace. The chance that Marshal Swearingen would pursue him that far was close to nothing, even though Pendergast had killed the bank tellers.

But the small streams flowing into the river had swelled and contributed more water than the riverbanks could handle. To go out on the river, even in a large boat, would be dangerous. Slocum knew the outlaw was caught here until the river crested and the flood had abated, which might be days.

He rode to the pier and looked out at the large riverboat banging against its moorings. A smile came to his lips. His guess was proving right. Now all he had to do was find Pendergast, and he had to admit Abe's dying words might have meant something else.

Slocum didn't think so.

He dismounted and walked to the buildings at the foot of the pier. A quick look through a dirty window showed only three men inside, none of them Pendergast or others of his gang.

As he went in, the man behind a long bar called out, "Ain't fixin' to leave for another day, maybe two. You want a drink to ease the wait?"

"Drink sounds good," Slocum said, dropping a damp greenback on the bar. It had been one of the bills he had taken from Abe and Herman. He thought Roebuck owed him a drink on the bank because he had already killed two of the robbers responsible for the tellers' deaths.

"Twice that. Don't like paper money. If you got coin . . ."

Slocum added another dollar bill to the one on the bar. The barkeep made a sour face, then made the money disappear and get replaced, as if my magic, with a shot glass brimming with a murky fluid resembling the muddy water in the river.

A sip confirmed Slocum's appraisal. It was terrible trade whiskey. Too much gunpowder and not enough alcohol. He knocked it back fast to keep from tasting it. He belched.

"Good, huh? Another?"

"Might as well since the boat's tied up for a while," Slocum said. The last thing in the world he needed was another drink. After the barkeep poured, Slocum let it sit on the bar, only fingering the shot glass to give the illusion of drinking. "You got other passengers waiting for it to leave?"

"A couple. Them gents," the barkeep said, pointing to the men playing gin rummy at a nearby table.

Slocum sized them up fast. One was a preacher and the other a traveling salesman.

"I was supposed to meet a fellow here," Slocum said.

"You just missed him then," the barkeep said. "The only other gent who wanted passage downriver left instead of stickin' around. Can't blame him. He looked to be in a powerful hurry to get somewhere that wasn't here."

"Do tell," Slocum said. "Might be the one I was waiting for."

"Don't remember much 'bout him. Big man, wore a gun like he knew how to use it." The bartender looked down at Slocum's six-gun, obviously putting him in the same bin as the other man. Gunfighters.

"He leave a name?"

"No need. He didn't buy a ticket but rode downstream. Ain't as fast as the boat, 'cept right now. But if he'd hung around a day or two, the boat'll sail on past wherever he got to."

"Could be he intends to get on the boat farther downstream," Slocum said.

"Kinda dumb wearin' out your horse when you could rest up here and enjoy our fine hospitality."

"Downstream?" Slocum asked.

"Didn't pay much attention, but if he wanted to buy a ticket on the boat, that's the only direction he'd go."

Slocum left the shot of whiskey on the bar and stepped back into the bright, cool day. Pendergast had intended to go as far as he could downriver, but the flood waters kept him from that. Slocum gathered his reins and stepped up, turned his horse upriver, and started riding. It took less than a half hour for him to confirm what he had thought Pendergast would do. Anyone on the outlaw's trail would assume he had ridden downstream. If the boat had set out when he had arrived, he would have gone that way since travel was faster on the water. Barring that, he wanted to avoid any possible pursuit since he had most of the loot.

Slocum picked up the pace. Pendergast couldn't be too much ahead of him. The barkeep had mentioned only the bank robber, though the rest of Pendergast's gang might have been with him but out of sight. Still, the more Slocum considered that, the less sense it made. Pendergast had intended to get away from his men, to steal their cut of the money except for his staunchest henchmen, Herman and

Abe. He might be running from the others in the gang as much as any posse on his trail.

His horse began to tire from the pace, so Slocum took a break, letting the horse dine on some new grass poking up from the muddy soil while he looked over the trail. He dropped to hands and knees and looked at the prints in the soft earth critically. He hoped to find a nick in one horseshoe to give a definite identification but nothing unusual showed. On hands and knees he examined another print and another, then stopped to consider what a new set of tracks might mean.

A rider had come from the direction of Central City. An outlaw? Marshal Swearingen? Slocum didn't think the marshal was the kind to send his entire posse back and press on after a fugitive all by his lonesome. If anything, Swearingen would offer more reward money and worry about paying it when they actually caught the gang.

A single rider. From the distance between the front and the rear hoofprints, the horse was galloping. After Pendergast. This made Slocum think another of Pendergast's henchmen had joined him. He stood and looked into the misty distance. He sucked in his breath. He had picked up the tracks of a scout Marshal Swearingen had sent out. The posse appeared as if by magic and homed in on him like they were bees and he was a pollen-laden flower.

"What you doin' out here?" The first rider held his shotgun across his lap as he rode up to Slocum.

"Where's the marshal?" Slocum looked at the six others who joined the first rider.

"He gave up, but we're after ourselves some bank robbers."

"I don't recognize any of you," Slocum said.

"We were just ridin' through when we heard 'bout the reward. We kin be real good citizens when that banker fellow—"

"Roebuck," Slocum supplied.

"—when that banker ponies up the reward. We got ourselves a description of the robber." He swung his shotgun around and pointed it at Slocum.

A cold chill passed through him as he stared down the twin barrels. These men didn't know that Magnuson and Norton had alibied him. He was likely to end up dead if he didn't convince them in a hurry he wasn't Pendergast.

"I work for Mr. Magnuson," Slocum said.

"Don't much care. Don't know this Magnuson, but we do know we're huntin' for a hat with a hatband made from snakeskin. Show us your hat."

Slocum stepped closer, aware of the knife's edge he walked between living and dying. He tipped his head down to give the bounty hunter a look at his Stetson.

"Mighty nice hat," the man said, "but it ain't the one we're lookin' for."

"Glad to hear that," Slocum said. He hooked his fingers through his gun belt, fingers pressing down on the top of the derringer he had taken from Abe. If things went south, he'd get at least one shot at the shotgun-wielding man.

"You know anything about a man with such a hatband?"

"The folks back at the river landing might. Downstream a few miles."

"Landing? There a boat?"

Slocum allowed as to how there was. All he wanted was this posse to let him be so he could run down Pendergast and finish his business with the outlaw. A few hours would be all he needed.

"Much obliged," the bounty hunter said. "We got ourselves a new trail to follow, men," he called. "If there's a boat, he must be headin' downstream."

Slocum watched them ride away. He slid the derringer back under his belt, heaved a deep sigh, then pulled his horse away from where it grazed. The horse tried to balk, but time pressed down on Slocum. He had seen the likes of the men in that posse—bounty hunters—and hated them with a grim, cold revulsion he could never put into words. They hunted men for money and seldom cared if the one they caught had a wanted poster nailed up somewhere. Slocum had been lucky that Roebuck probably had demanded the return of the hat for them to claim their reward.

The horse settled down, and Slocum pressed on as fast as he could, eyeing the twin tracks in the ground. Did they ride together or was Pendergast in the lead and the other trailed him? He had no way to tell.

Slocum drew rein and turned his head to the side when he thought he heard a gunshot. It was faint, distant, possibly something other than gunfire. Then he heard three more quick shots. Not knowing what he was getting into, he galloped ahead, found that the bank of the river had vanished and left a floodplain. He cut away from the water and rode toward a distant stand of trees that poked up like a pimple on a young kid's nose.

No more shots rang out. Slocum checked his six-shooter as he rode. Six rounds. He drew his rifle and made certain it carried a full magazine. Then he slowed and approached the woods with more caution than was necessary. Only a few yards into the copse he saw bare feet sticking out, toes down.

He rode over to where Pendergast lay dead as a doornail. He had been stripped down to his long johns. His boots were gone, as was every stitch of clothing, including his hat.

"The damned hat," Slocum said. It was the key to releasing the reward money.

"You wanted to kill him yourself, didn't you, Slocum?"

He whirled, rifle coming up. Slocum hesitated when he saw that Tom Garvin had the drop on him. A moment's shock stayed his finger on the Winchester's trigger and gave Garvin the chance to swing his black rope like a whip.

Slocum winced as the rope curled around his wrist. Garvin yanked and sent the rifle pinwheeling through the air. It crashed to the ground and discharged.

"You was gonna shoot me, weren't you?" Garvin snapped the rope one-handed, and it responded like a thing alive. He held his six-shooter in his other hand to keep Slocum from going for his own gun.

"Looks like you beat me to Pendergast."

"I took a shine to his clothes. He was a snappy dresser, but things is a bit large." Slocum would have laughed as Garvin held out his arms to show how he had rolled up the sleeves. His pant legs were turned up like a sodbuster with a new pair of overalls, and he had Pendergast's hat tipped back on his head.

Slocum's hand slipped slowly toward his left hip, but Garvin aimed his pistol straight at him.

"I think it might be interestin' to kill you, Slocum. You hate me, and I don't know why."

"You brought Pendergast down with your first shot." Slocum glanced over at the body. "The next three went into his back."

"That 'bout sums it up," Garvin said, grinning wickedly. "He mighta been alive. Just wanted to make certain."

"You enjoyed shooting him in the back."

"So?" Garvin circled to get behind Slocum.

As Magnuson's new foreman moved, Slocum reached under his belt and pressed the derringer into the palm of his hand.

"Drop that gun belt of yours, Slocum. Make a move for the six-shooter and you're as dead as that son-of-a-bitch bank robber."

"You took his gear, too. You're getting to be quite a thief, Garvin."

"Ain't doin' him no good. And that's a powerful lot of money from the bank. Considerin' what to do with it. Why, I might salt it away and make a play for that purty little filly that throwed you."

Slocum tensed. Garvin laughed at his reaction.

"What can Josh Norton offer her I can't? He might meet

a sad end, and if I was there to comfort her, why, she might decide to up and marry me. I could use the bank robbery money to buy into the Bar M. That'd set me up real good."

Slocum had nothing to say. He coughed to cover his move, pulling back the hammer on the derringer.

"Where'd you ride in from, Slocum? You followin' the riverbank?"

"Came from a riverboat depot."

"Do tell." Garvin paused a moment, then laughed. "You're a mighty smart cayuse, Slocum. Pendergast wanted to use it as a way to escape, but the river's too high."

"That's the way it was," Slocum said. "But you found Pendergast first. How?"

"Just part of my good luck." Garvin moved more to position himself completely behind Slocum. "I have good and then bad, but right now I'm ridin' high."

Slocum twisted around, thrust out his gun hand, and fired. The derringer's slug tore into Garvin and staggered him. Then he recovered and opened fire. Slocum wasted no time bringing his horse to a gallop to get the hell away. Garvin kept firing until Slocum was far away.

Working his way through the wooded area, he came out on the river and looked back. The posse of bounty hunters hadn't taken his bait and were riding hard for the woods. Slocum wanted to settle accounts with Garvin, but he knew that tangling with the bounty hunters wasn't a good idea. He clutched the derringer with its single round remaining, then pressed his hand to his left hip, where his Colt ought to have ridden. He wasn't going to leave his six-shooter back there with Tom Garvin.

Taking a wide circle of the woods, he heard rapid gunfire, then nothing. Trying to count the rounds wasn't possible because the shots had been spaced so closely together that it sounded like one huge report, almost howitzer-like in intensity.

He hesitated, then dismounted and sat on a rock, staring

into the woods as if he could see through the tree trunks and undergrowth. After a few minutes, he got too antsy, mounted, and rode straight to the spot where he had shot it out with Tom Garvin.

He drew rein and stared. For a moment he thought Garvin was still alive. The black rope tied around his neck twitched and writhed as if it were alive, but the man couldn't have been. His hands had been tied behind his back and his feet dangled three feet from the ground.

His hat with the fancy snakeskin hatband was missing. The bounty hunters had their proof they had found the bank robber. It was Garvin's bad luck he had stolen the one thing that identified him as Pendergast.

"Good luck and bad. This is the worst luck you're ever going to have," Slocum muttered. He rode around the slowly swinging body, found where his gun belt lay, and retrieved it. Once it was snugged down around his waist, he felt like he could whip his weight in wildcats.

He considered going after the bounty hunters because they weren't likely to admit to finding the loot from the bank robbery. They would try to bilk Roebuck out of both the stolen money and the reward on Pendergast's head. He could do that, maybe save Roebuck a few dollars. He could return to the Bar M and have it out with Christine.

John Slocum mounted and rode back to the pier. A ride downstream on the riverboat was the best idea he could come up with because it got him the hell away from everything.

21

The circling buzzards bothered Willie Wilson. The rain had made travel awful the past few days, but he intended to get downriver, eventually following the swollen stream that fed into the bigger one. He'd heard tell there was a riverboat that would take him a considerable distance faster than he could ride, but he didn't have two nickels to rub together. Shaking some droplets of rainwater from his yellow slicker, he used his bandanna to dry his face. The way the buzzards spiraled downward told him something had died not too far off.

He had a lot of vices, and curiosity might be his worst since he had finished off the pint of brandy that had served him over the miles, he'd run out of tobacco days earlier, and there wasn't anything female within miles.

His horse shied as he started through the woods. He found a game trail and followed that to an area that hardly deserved the name of clearing. The sight that greeted him caused his belly to clench up.

A man had been hanged. Crows had already pecked out his eyes and other choice tidbits, and now the vultures were coming to pick the carcass clean.

"Git outta here!" He drew his six-shooter and fired a round to scare off the carrion birds. They looked at him with cold hatred in their beady red eyes and then took to wing, running clumsily a few feet and then launching into the air.

The body was past identification. The face was pecked and destroyed by insects. The one thing Willie noticed was the black rope that had been used as a noose. It was ebon-black with silver threads chased through it.

"Now that's a real purty rope," he said to himself. Willie grunted as he reached over and lifted the body up. To his surprise, the rope uncurled from around the dead man's neck and hung loose from the tree limb.

He dropped the body and grabbed the rope.

"Ouch!" He pulled back from it. "Damned thing bit me." He looked at his hand but saw no wound. Bending over, he snared it and pulled it off the tree limb. "How about that?"

The rope coiled itself easily and felt *right* in his hand. He spun it a few times, liking the ease with which he kept the loop open. Roping calves would be easy with it. A quick twist of his wrist brought the rope to his knee, where he fastened it to the saddle.

Willie looked down at the body, considered giving it a decent burial, then rode off. He didn't have any idea what words to say over a grave, and besides, the birds and bugs had started picking off the putrid flesh. Let them dine.

He reached down, touched the rope, and felt a glow of pride, of accomplishment, of power. With this he could be the best cowpuncher ever. Willie Wilson rode on, humming to himself.

Watch for

SLOCUM AND THE TRICK SHOT ARTIST

402nd novel in the exciting SLOCUM series
from Jove

Coming in August!